USA TODAY bestselling author **Heidi Rice** lives in London, England. She is married with two teenage sons—which gives her rather too much of an insight into the male psyche—and also works as a film journalist. She adores her job, which involves getting swept up in a world of high emotions, sensual excitement, funny, feisty women, sexy, tortured men and glamorous locations where laundry doesn't exist. Once she turns off her computer she often does chores—usually involving laundry!

Also by Heidi Rice

Too Close for Comfort
One Night, So Pregnant!
Vows They Can't Escape
The Virgin's Shock Baby
Captive at Her Enemy's Command

Discover more at millsandboon.co.uk.

BOUND BY THEIR SCANDALOUS BABY

HEIDI RICE

MILLS & BOON

First Published in Great Britain 2018
by Mills & Boon, an imprint of HarperCollins*Publishers*
1 London Bridge Street, London, SE1 9GF

© 2018 Heidi Rice

ISBN: 978-0-263-93479-3

MIX
Paper from
responsible sources
FSC C007454

This book is produced from independently certified FSC™ paper
to ensure responsible forest management.
For more information visit www.harpercollins.co.uk/green.

Printed and bound in Spain
by CPI, Barcelona

To Sharon Kendrick,
for being an inspiration and a friend.

CHAPTER ONE

LUKAS BLACKSTONE HATED CROWDS. But he hated dark rooms a whole lot more. Tonight, he would have to endure both at the same time. A humiliating trickle of sweat eased down his temple. He brushed it away impatiently with the cuff of his tuxedo jacket. The tailored designer suit felt like a straitjacket, squeezing the air out of his lungs. The irrational fear made his stomach knot.

He cast a jaundiced eye over the array of VIP guests below him—crammed into the Art Deco ballroom of Blackstone's Manhattan, his company's flagstone hotel on the corner of Central Park West.

Hollywood A-listers bumped shoulders with masters of industry, legendary rock stars mingled with media moguls, priceless jewellery sparkled and glowed, and vintage champagne flowed alongside a lavish buffet of delicacies produced by an award-winning chef. A thirty-piece orchestra brought the closing strains of a Viennese waltz to an end. Blackstone's Full Moon Ball was the classiest event of the season. There was more money on display tonight than the GDP of most European countries, but to Lukas, unlike his twin brother Alexei, it had always looked like a seething mass of humanity ready to swallow him whole.

'Don't sweat it, bro. You don't want to dance in the

dark with one of these babes, I've got this. But don't come crying to me when I score and you don't.'

His brother's voice, smug and irreverent and full of the reckless charm that had made Alexei irresistible to women the world over, whispered across Lukas's consciousness. A leaden weight joined the tangle of nerves in his belly.

He sunk his fists into the pockets of his suit pants and let the moment of loss wash over him as he stared down at the ballroom floor. The cloying cloud of expensive perfumes and colognes rose to the mezzanine level where he stood, concealed from prying eyes.

'Mr Blackstone, sir. Mr Garvey wants to know if you've picked your partner for the Dark Waltz?'

Lukas swung round to see one of his publicity chief Dex Garvey's minions. He glanced at his watch. Ten to twelve. *Damn.*

He pushed the shadow of reminiscence to one side. He had to make an appearance on the ballroom floor at midnight—when the lights would be dimmed—and claim a woman to dance alone with her, creating a spectacle for the press which had been a highlight of the Ball since the Roaring Twenties.

It was a tradition started by his great-grandfather—a murderous Russian bootlegger—who had used the first Blackstone Full Moon Ball as a uniquely barbaric way to claim his unsuspecting bride from the debutantes of New York high society.

Unfortunately, Dex Garvey had decided Lukas could do the same.

'Tell Garvey it's none of his business,' he barked. The minion took the hint and scurried off.

Irritated by the need to make a public spectacle of himself, and the tight knots still competing with the hollow ache in his stomach, he scanned the dance floor for a suitable candidate as the Dark Waltz was announced and the eligible women gathered in the centre of the room.

He ignored the cluster of girls from some of Europe and America's best families. He knew Garvey had invited them in the hope he would choose one to create a buzz around the planted story about his supposed search for a wife—as Blackstone's prepared to open its first luxury family resort on a private atoll in the Maldives.

The move into the family market was a sound business decision, nothing more—a chance to consolidate Blackstone's as the leading luxury brand in all sectors of the global hospitality industry—but Lukas had absolutely no intention of becoming a family man himself just to promote it.

The knots in his stomach tightened as he left his sanctuary and descended the staircase. A sea of eager female faces watched him. The opening bars of the Dark Waltz drowned out the hum of anticipation from the crowd—and the rush of blood in his ears—when his gaze landed on a young woman standing alone.

Unlike the others, who waited with barely concealed anticipation at the thought that he might pick them, she stood apart, her stance brittle and guarded.

The jolt of awareness hit him. Her slender body was temptingly displayed in a green satin gown, its classic style a lot simpler than the expensive designer gowns of the other women. Pale alabaster skin was offset by a mass of wild red curls swept up in a haphazard style that made him itch to tug away the pins keeping it aloft.

As the lights dimmed, the girl's skin took on an ethereal glow in the moonlight and he got close enough to make out her features. The visceral blast of heat was followed by the shock of recognition.

Darcy O'Hara. The girl who had attempted to black-mail Alexei four years ago—just before his death. What the hell was she doing in New York?

He recoiled, fury and loss strangling him. But he couldn't halt his steps or change direction as he strode across the floor towards her. A barrage of camera flashes went off around him like fireworks and the other women faded into the background—because the only woman he could focus on was her.

The knots of tension released in a rush, setting off a chain reaction throughout his body, the predatory instinct like a drug.

She tensed, her gaze fixed on his, and her body trembled as if she were poised to run—like a gazelle scenting a panther stalking her in the long grass.

But she stood her ground.

He would have given her points for that, except he didn't buy the shocked and fragile act for a second. The sharp sweet taste of revenge overrode the familiar childhood fear that had dogged him for years as the darkness descended. The full moon's beams through the ballroom's glass ceiling provided the only illumination. The anxiety burned away on the focused wave of fury and the inexplicable flare of desire.

You should have run, Darcy, because you're not going to like what happens next.

Reaching her at last, he grasped one narrow wrist in an iron grip and wrapped his other arm around her slender waist to yank her towards him.

Without asking permission, he swung her into a turn as the music began, trapping her against his body. She arched back against his restraining arm, the cello strings marking the beat. He could hear the gasp of distress, feel the shudder of her rapid breathing, the softness of her skin as his palm strayed down to where the gown's back plunged low.

Holding her insultingly close, he forced her to follow his lead.

He didn't care if he was treating her like a whore. Because that was exactly what she was.

Darcy O'Hara was going to pay for the lies she'd told Alexei, not to mention her decision to gatecrash this event. By the end of this dance, every single member of the paparazzi in Manhattan would know what a manipulative little gold-digger she was—because he planned to give the world's press and every person here a graphic demonstration.

'Mr Blackstone…' she stuttered, the crisp English accent smokier than he remembered from their one brief meeting, as she struggled against his hold. 'You're hurting me,' she said breathlessly.

He loosened his grip, but only enough to ensure he didn't bruise her. He wasn't the monster here—she was.

'Call me Lukas,' he snarled, thinking of Alexei—irresponsible, impulsive and far too easily fooled by a pretty face—and all he'd lost the day this woman had worked her way into his brother's bed and messed with his head. 'And stop wriggling.'

Bronte O'Hara's head spun, her confusion almost as huge as her panic, as Lukas Blackstone's arms closed around her like steel bands.

But as her brain knotted, trying to make sense of what had just happened, her body burned—so powerfully aware of this man she had never met before, further protests got lodged in her throat.

He whisked her around the floor, the kaleidoscope of flashing lights and sound whirling past her in giddying circles. Her skin stretched tight over her bones, and her breasts swelled in the too-tight bodice of the gown she'd found in a thrift store in the East Village the day before—so she could gatecrash this event and meet this man who might well be her nephew's only hope. She'd already known Lukas Blackstone was a bastard, after the way he'd treated Darcy four years ago. Even so, she'd been prepared to beg him for his help, for his attention—but she hadn't expected this.

The possessive press of one large hand scalded the base of her spine, her senses overwhelmed by the irresistible fragrance of juniper and pine from his cologne and his own musky scent.

She felt trapped, controlled, completely at his mercy. She'd never danced a waltz before in her life, but his confident, fluid steps made it impossible for her to stumble, her feet barely touching the ground.

The music built to a crescendo, her breathing becoming ragged, and her exhausted mind seemed no longer capable of engaging with anything but the sight and sound of him. The moonlight made it feel as if she were being propelled in a dream—a terrifyingly erotic dream—her body becoming one throbbing, pulsating bundle of nerve-endings. Through the maelstrom of conflicting emotions, her mind clung desperately to one coherent thought.

She hated this man, for everything he was and everything he stood for, and for everything he had done to Darcy and had tried to do to Nico. Four years ago, he'd attempted to bribe her sister into aborting his brother's child.

But why then did she feel so alive in his arms? It was as if a veil had been ripped away to expose her, naked and yearning, the minute he had marched towards her and dragged her into his embrace.

Why did her body revel in his punishing hold? Why did

she feel this desperate compulsion to rub against the un-yielding lines of his powerful physique? Why did her lungs want to pull in greedy breaths of that intoxicating scent?

After what felt like an eternity, but could only have been a few minutes, the glide of violin and cello, the flut-ter of piccolo and flute faded into silence and they came to an abrupt standstill.

She could hear her own rapid breathing as her body hummed with a thousand tiny pinpricks of agonised sen-sation. Abruptly he let her go. She stumbled and his hand clamped around her upper arm.

Applause erupted around them. She heard his vicious curse, then suddenly she was in his arms again. But this time his lips were on hers, his tongue demanding entry. She opened for him instinctively, her gasp cut off as his tongue swept inside.

Strong fingers plunged into her hair, the stinging in her scalp as the pins scattered nothing compared to the brutal blaze of sensation firing up from her core.

Overcome, overwhelmed, she was unable to control her desperate, wanton response to the kiss. Part of her mind knew this was a punishment—she could feel his contempt, taste his disgust—but as he held her head and pillaged her mouth she was powerless to resist the heat firing through every one of those newly awakened nerve-endings.

She felt dazed, giddy with pleasure, as the darkness began to lift. But then he thrust her away from him. The applause had died, to be replaced with hissed whispers, taut silence.

She got her first proper look at the face that had haunted her for over three years. But he looked nothing like the pictures she'd seen of his brother. His identical twin. His dark onyx eyes glittered with heat and con-tempt. The scar that ran in an arc down the left side of his face mesmerised her for one crucial second—she had read he'd acquired the disfiguring injury in a childhood accident—but the wound which had marred the perfect symmetry of his features had turned what should have been a classically handsome face into something brooding and intense and a million times more compelling.

She pressed her fingers to her lips, which felt tender from the pressure of his kiss, and watched as if in a trance as his sensual lips moved.

'I see you're still the same little whore who seduced my brother,' he said, his voice so low she almost couldn't hear it above the rumble of speculation from the crowd.

The words exploded in her head, shattering the moment of stunned arousal, as he clicked his fingers above his head, signalling the security guards she'd been dodging all evening.

Fear and anger, and disgust—with herself as much as him—combined in the pit of her stomach and her fist shot out.

The thud of the punch sounded like canon fire. She heard the muscles in his neck pop as his head snapped back—and pain exploded in her knuckles.

'Your brother was the whore,' she shouted. 'Not Darcy.'

Hard hands grabbed her from behind. She struggled against the security guard's hold.

'Get her out of here and hand her over to the police,' Blackstone said as he tested his jaw.

Her hand throbbed but he looked barely fazed by the punch as he flicked a contemptuous glance down her body, then turned and walked away.

'Wait, wait!' she shouted as the guard hefted her backwards, the crowd in an uproar. But Blackstone didn't even glance back.

Nico. What have I done?

Horror at her impulsiveness fired through her.

She'd spent the last of her savings, and precious days, trying to contact this man. Had used every last ounce of the ingenuity and bravery she possessed to set up this one chance to meet him. And now she'd blown it in a matter of minutes because of one insane dance and a mind-blowing kiss.

The despair that had dogged her for weeks—months— ever since her nephew had been diagnosed with a rare form of blood cancer threatened to descend, as the security guard kept a tight arm around her midriff.

She was going to be arrested, kicked out of the US, possibly even remanded in custody. Lukas Blackstone would take out a restraining order against her and Nico would have no one. And no chance.

Mustering the last of her strength, she kicked hard against the security guard's shin. He dumped her on the ground with a muffled curse. Scrambling up, she raced through the phalanx of photographers after Blackstone, who was heading back towards the stairs he had come down, clearly intending to leave the dance floor as abruptly as he had arrived.

She grabbed his sleeve, tugged as hard as she could, her knuckles still stinging from connecting with a jaw harder than granite. He jerked round, the livid red mark on his chin taunting her.

'I'm not Darcy. I'm her sister. Darcy's dead—she died three years ago. But I have to speak to you about her son. Nico is Alexei's son too. I… *Oof.*'

The hard arm of the security guard locked round her tummy again, with bruising force this time, but as she was hauled back, Blackstone raised his hand. 'Put her down.'

She was dropped to her feet. She staggered and would

have fallen, but for the iron grip as his hand snagged her upper arm.

'What did you say?' Blackstone demanded.

She's lying.

Lukas fought to regain his cast-iron control. And locate the cold hard logic he relied on which had deserted him the minute he'd set eyes on the woman. But as he held the girl's slender arm, watched her pulse batter her collarbone and studied her heart-shaped face, seeing the anguish and defiance in her vivid emerald eyes, the sprinkle of freckles across her nose, the full lips reddened by his angry kiss—one realisation blindsided him.

This girl was not the woman who had disturbed his brother's mind with her insidious lies four years ago. The shape of her face was different; she was slightly shorter—and she had none of Darcy O'Hara's guile.

Strangely, the knowledge quelled at least a little of his fury.

He would have hated himself if he had responded to Darcy in that way. If she were really dead, he certainly felt no regret. But then he registered what else the girl had said. She was Darcy's sister, and still peddling the same damn lie her sister Darcy had used four years ago to extort money from Alexei.

So was his attraction to this girl really any better?

He shouldn't have touched her, certainly shouldn't have kissed her. But the compulsion to teach her a lesson had become mixed up in a host of unbidden and unwanted desires as her fresh, subtle scent had engulfed him and her body had surrendered to his during the steps of the dance.

One look at those damn lips as they'd finished dancing, her panting breaths making her full breasts rise and fall against the bodice of her gown—and all he'd wanted to do was feast on her mouth.

He didn't like it. He mastered his urges. Controlled them. Unlike his brother, he had learned at an early age that impulse and need were a weakness, and dangerous if you indulged either one. But he'd never had that control tested until about five minutes ago, when he'd spied her in the crowd. Instincts beyond his control had taken over at that point. It was something he would have to examine carefully after he was finished with her—because he did not intend to let it happen again.

'Please, you have to listen to me,' she begged, even though the flash of defiance in her eyes told a different story.

He felt a certain admiration for her. She might be as much of a gold-digger as her sister, but she had none of Darcy's acting ability—her enmity towards him was plain on her face.

'I have to do no such thing,' he said. But he didn't let go of her arm. Instead he walked towards the staircase, hauling her with him—the crowd already closing in on him.

'Mr Blackstone, the police are on their way.' Jack Tanner, the head of his security team for Blackstone's Manhattan, fell into step on his other side, looking ill at ease.

And well he should.

'Find out how she got past security,' he barked, fuming at that oversight. 'I want a full report on my desk in an hour.'

'Yes, sir,' Tanner replied. 'Do you want us to take her off your hands?' he offered, two of his security detail following close behind as they mounted the stairs.

The girl hadn't objected to being marched out of the ballroom, but he felt her stiffen at the suggestion.

Pausing at the top of the stairs, he could see the paparazzi firing off shots from behind the security cordon and Dex Garvey having a microphone shoved in his face. The eyes of the guests were on them. This little incident was going to be all over the gossip columns in the morning and would already have started hitting the celebrity blogs and websites. He'd helped with that—by not resisting the foolish urge to dance with her, and then kiss her—but the icing on the cake would be the girl's fatuous claim about Alexei having a child.

The pulse of loss hit him hard. And then fury reverberated through him. He'd make sure she paid for that piece of theatre. He had no doubt at all she'd been waiting for an opportunity to announce the lie at a moment when it would get maximum exposure—to increase the price of her silence and her bargaining position. That he'd gifted her the perfect photo op with that kiss only made him more furious, with himself as much as her.

This girl was about to find out that he could not be as easily manipulated as he had been four years ago, when he'd parted with fifty thousand dollars simply to save Alexei the embarrassment of having to make a public announcement that he was not responsible for Darcy's so-called condition.

Well, Alexei was gone now—the car crash that had killed him while he was out of his head on cocaine and champagne a direct result of Darcy O'Hara's lies, to Lukas's way of thinking. So Lukas had no reason and certainly no incentive to pay another cent. But this girl needed to be taught a lesson. Once and for all.

He wasn't leaving that task to the police or anyone else. He owed it to Alexei.

'I wish to talk to her in private,' he said to Tanner. 'Keep the police busy until then. And get rid of the press.'

He would speak to Garvey tomorrow about a press release to quell any rumours arising from this evening's events. Alexei had always wanted to avoid just such a necessity, but Alexei was gone now. And the truth could no longer hurt him. If anything, it ought to stop any more gold-diggers like the O'Hara sisters coming out of the woodwork.

He felt the girl's body sag, no doubt with relief. As he marched her down the corridor towards his private suite he felt an answering surge of satisfaction. She thought she'd just got what she wanted. He was going to enjoy proving the opposite.

He entered the suite and hauled her in after him, then let her go. As she stumbled to a stop in the centre of the room, he slammed the door and clicked the lock.

He shoved his hands into his pockets, angered anew by the pulse of heat in his crotch which hadn't subsided since that ill-advised kiss.

She wrapped her arms around her midriff, the tremors racking her body a nice touch, he thought, as she lifted her chin and faced him, the leap of defiance still sparkling in the green depths of her irises. Her freckles stood out against the vivid flush of exertion on her cheeks—but he noticed for the first time the shadows under her eyes.

He ruthlessly quelled the prickle of sympathy.

Maybe she was an even better actress than her sister, after all. From the look of her, anyone would think she was an avenging angel on the verge of collapse, not an accomplished little blackmailer.

His gaze roamed over her, and he let every ounce of his contempt show. In the brighter light, the dress looked considerably less impressive. It didn't even fit her properly, the soft mounds of her breasts pressed indecently against the satin. His gaze snagged on the outline of her nipples. He jerked it away again, before the heat in his crotch swelled.

She'd lost her shoes in the struggle with the security guard, her bare unpainted toes peeping out from underneath the gown's frayed hem.

His gaze rose to examine her face. She wore no jewellery and minimal make-up. Her dewy skin was as soft and clear as a child's. He flinched inwardly—exactly how old was she? She looked like a teenager, eighteen or nineteen at the most, playing dress-up.

The Little Orphan Annie look wasn't one he'd been susceptible to before now—which only made the incendiary effect of having her in his arms, her mouth at his mercy, all the more galling and inexplicable.

'Talk,' he said. The curt demand made her flinch. 'You've got five minutes to explain exactly how much you think your little revelation about Alexei fathering a son is worth before I hand you over to the cops.'

At which point he would take great pleasure in adding a charge of extortion to the ones of trespass and assault.

'What?' Bronte's voice broke on the word, her shock almost as huge as her exhaustion. And her confusion.

'You heard me. How. Much.' The jagged scar on his cheek pulsed, emphasising his hatred.

And, as much as she hated him in return, she didn't understand it.

Exactly how cruel and arrogant was this man? She'd just told him his dead twin had a child. And all he seemed concerned about was money—and humiliating her.

He'd treated her with complete contempt, from the moment he'd laid eyes on her. He'd as good as ravaged her in front of hundreds of people—and said the most vile things imaginable about a woman who couldn't defend herself—and now he was accusing her of being some kind of blackmailer.

She bit into her lip, hard enough to taste blood. And held on to the diatribe she wanted to scream at him.

Don't punch him again, Bronte. You need his co-operation. Nico needs his cooperation.

She flexed her fingers, pressing the bruised knuckles under her arm, and tried to channel Mahatma Gandhi. Not easy when she was feeling more like Genghis Khan.

Unfortunately, Lukas Blackstone was the one with all the power here. Not just in terms of his money and influence, but even within the confines of this room. He towered over her. In her bare feet she was barely five foot three; she suspected he was at least a foot taller, with an impressively fit build for a man who had probably spent every moment of his existence being pampered to within an inch of his life. There wasn't an ounce of softness or give about him. He looked completely indomitable—and completely furious. Like a lion in his prime—who could devour her and all her hopes with one vicious swipe of his paw, and then forget about her.

'I don't want your money,' she said, as clearly as she could while her knees were shaking.

She wasn't scared of him, she told herself staunchly. This was just a reaction to everything that had happened in the last few minutes, and hours, and days and weeks. It felt as if all her hopes and fears, all her dreams and all her nightmares, were centred in this one room, concentrated on this one man—and, for better or worse, she had to come out on top in this battle of wills or she would lose everything that mattered to her.

Unfortunately, she had never been the sunny, flirtatious, irresistible sister. That had always been Darcy. Darcy with her sweet smile and her effervescent laugh and her determination to always see the best in people, even the father who had discarded them both to start another family. And Alexei Blackstone, who Darcy had been convinced had fallen madly in love with her, even if all the evidence from their one-night stand and its aftermath had suggested the opposite.

Alexei Blackstone had used Darcy. He'd been nothing more than a billionaire playboy who had hooked up with her sister for a night in Monaco, while her sister had been working at the casino bar and he'd been touring the tables. After a moonlit drive in his new sports car, he'd seduced her hopelessly romantic sister over champagne and canapés in the Blackstone Villa on the Côte D'Azur. He'd taken her virginity and then discarded her the next day. Darcy had lost her job and returned to London, confused and heartbroken, but when she'd found out she was pregnant, contacting Alexei had been impossible. He'd never responded to any of the frantic messages Darcy had left him. And then Lukas had appeared in London a few days later, his limousine taking Darcy to a private meeting at the Blackstone Park Lane. There he'd tried to bully and blackmail Darcy into having an abortion, which Darcy had been convinced had all been Lukas's idea.

Bronte wasn't convinced that Alexei wasn't the one who had set his big brother on Darcy and told him to bribe her into silence, but Darcy wouldn't hear of it.

Alexei Blackstone was as much of a creep as his brother to Bronte's way of thinking—just a more charming one. But when Darcy had spoken of him that last time, months after his death, her eyes glazed with fever and love, an hour after Nico's birth, Bronte had simply nodded, having lost the desire to destroy her sister's comforting delusions.

'Promise me you won't tell Alexei's brother I didn't have the abortion. Lukas must never know about Nico.'

Bronte's mind stalled, the fog of exhaustion burned away by the flash fire of memory. She flexed her fingers, feeling Darcy's weak grip tightening on her hand as the sharp sickly smell of morphine and disinfectant clogged Bronte's lungs. And the words that had haunted her and driven her for three years whispered across her consciousness.

'I promise, Darcy. I'll look after Nico. And Lukas Blackstone will never know he exists.'

She'd only been eighteen when Nico had come into her life and the double whammy of responsibility and Darcy's death had cut her carefree existence off at the knees. The newborn baby had been nothing but a burden at first, especially in the depths of her grief, when just getting out of bed each morning had felt like an endeavour on a par with building the Taj Mahal singlehanded.

But eventually Nico, such a sweet, smiley baby boy, had become Bronte's salvation, yanking her out of her grief and back into the world. She'd found a secure job as a nightclub cleaner and worked her backside off to raise Nico alone. And eventually she and Nico had found a rhythm. A rhythm which suited them. They'd weathered the highs and the many lows together. They were a team. And she'd kept her promise to Darcy. Until Nico's paediatrician Dr Patel had told her two days ago—in her bright airy office at Westminster Children's Hospital—that Bronte wasn't the donor they needed for Nico's treatment. And maybe they should look for a donor in his father's family.

Unlike Darcy, Bronte had always been a realist, a pragmatist, the one who knew people rarely, if ever, were as good as they appeared to be on the surface. And if she'd ever been an optimist she wasn't one any more. But if the paediatrician had believed the devil himself was Nico's best hope she would have tracked him down—and forced him to cooperate. But having to dig deep and find a way to charm Lukas Blackstone now she'd found him felt impossible somehow—probably because her experience of charming any man was precisely zilch.

Just concentrate on the now. And get through this. For Nikky and Darcy.

Lukas's brows drew down, making his harsh, brooding face look even more forbidding.

'If you don't want money,' he said, the cynical note a clear indication he was humouring her with that supposition, 'then why did you gatecrash this event?'

'I told you why,' Bronte snapped, then wished she could bite off her tongue. But he didn't seem particularly fazed by her show of temper. Probably because he held all the cards. 'Because I need to talk to you about Nico,' she continued. 'Who is your brother Alexei's son.'

Lukas's eyes flickered with an intense emotion she couldn't name. But then the tiny reaction was gone, and the look he sent her could only be described as scathing. And dismissive.

She pushed against the despair threatening to engulf her. Had coming here been a terrible mistake?

'Nico is your nephew,' she reiterated, even though admitting the connection between this cynical, indifferent man and that innocent, funny, beautiful little boy made her stomach hurt. 'He's only three years old and he's very ill—his only hope is an experimental stem cell treatment. We need at least a partial donor match but, with both his biological parents dead, Dr Patel says his best hope of finding a match is you—because you're his father's identical twin.'

Her voice trailed off because his face had remained impassive. Except for the tiny tic of a muscle in his jaw. Exactly how inhuman was he, that the plight of a child—his brother's child—wouldn't move him, even in the slightest?

But then his frown became more pronounced, as if he were considering what she'd said. Had he heard her? Would he at least consider helping?

'If there even is such a child,' he said, his tone laced with scepticism now as well as barely concealed contempt, 'and he is actually sick, I think we both know there is no chance I will be a suitable donor.'

'No, we don't. How could we? If you haven't been tested.'

'Because there is no possible way Alexei could have fathered this boy. Something your sister knew when she tried to claim the same thing four years ago.'

'Why are you saying that?' she asked, confused now as well as frightened. 'You *knew* Alexei was the father, or you wouldn't have given my sister fifty thousand dollars to have an abortion.'

His eyebrows rose then, and for the first time she could see she'd surprised him. 'Is that what your sister told you?'

'Yes, and I believed her—she would never have lied to me.' Darcy had never had a single duplicitous or greedy bone in her body. She'd taken this man's blood money, yes, but only for the sake of her child—to put a down payment on the tiny basement flat where they lived in Hackney, East London.

'How melodramatic,' he said. 'I didn't tell her to have an abortion, for the simple reason that I didn't believe her story about being pregnant. And if she was pregnant I knew damn well the child wasn't Alexei's. If she thought that was what the money was for, that was her interpretation. I simply told her I was paying her the money to rid myself and Alexei of the problem she presented.'

'But she *was* pregnant and Alexei *is* the father…'

'I met your sister exactly once,' Lukas interrupted, the contempt in his voice slicing Bronte to the bone. 'Obviously I underestimated the problem. I thought she was simply a good liar, an accomplished gold-digger. I didn't realise she was delusional and that she actually believed Alexei was the father.'

'But Darcy wasn't delusional. She was telling the truth.'

'No, she wasn't. Alexei could not possibly have fathered her child.'

'Why not?'

'Because my brother was infertile. He had been since the age of sixteen.'

'But that can't be true.' Bronte's mind stalled, the revelation a crushing blow. Had Darcy made a mistake? About Nico's father? Had this mission all been a pointless, futile exercise which was likely to get her arrested for no good reason…?

'I assure you it is true. My father got it on good authority from a number of specialists after a bout of mumps caused severe inflammation of Alexei's testes as a teenager.' The stormy expression on Lukas's face lifted the veil of indifference—so he did care, about his brother at least.

Bronte ignored the biting anger in his tone and struggled to get her head around this revelation. What Lukas was saying simply didn't stack up.

Alexei had been Darcy's first lover—her only lover. Clearly Lukas believed what he was saying about his brother. Which would explain why Lukas had offered Darcy money to get rid of her, and Alexei had refused to answer her calls. Obviously the two of them had both thought Darcy was some kind of conniving gold-digger looking for a pay-off, and they'd wanted to protect Alexei's pride. The fifty thousand dollars hadn't been to pay for an abortion, as Darcy in her panic and confusion had obviously assumed; it had simply been to stop her from going public with the news of a pregnancy they both believed Alexei could not have been responsible for.

But how did any of that explain why Nico looked so much like the Blackstone brothers? And how could Darcy possibly have got pregnant by someone else? If she'd never slept with another man?

Whatever Lukas Blackstone believed, he had to be wrong. Because Alexei had to be Nico's father. And that meant Lukas was still Nico's best chance of a donor.

'I don't care if the whole world thought your brother was infertile. He wasn't, because Nico is his son. Darcy said so, and you only have to look at him to know it's true.'

Lukas's face hardened, the tic in his jaw going berserk. The lion was about to pounce, but she didn't care any more; she would prod and provoke him until he accepted the truth—and gave Nico a chance.

'Clearly you're as much of a fantasist as your sister.' He drew a mobile phone out of his pocket and began to key in a number as he spoke. 'Your time's up, Miss O'Hara, and this farce is over.' He lifted the phone to his ear.

'Stop!' She grabbed his arm, horrified by the spurt of heat that snaked up her torso at the feel of his muscular forearm tensing beneath the sleeve of his tuxedo. 'Before you have me arrested. Just stop and think for a moment. What if the doctors were wrong? What if, by some miracle, your brother *did* father a child and Nico is all that's left of him?'

'I don't believe in miracles,' he said flatly, not surprising her in the slightest, but then he lowered the phone.

'Neither did I...' she said, because she hadn't until this very second, but she could see the spark of irritation—

and she thanked God for it, because it was enough to give him pause. 'Let me show you a photo of Nico,' she said, pouring the last of her hope into the plea. 'I've got loads of them on my phone—which is in my bag hidden behind the industrial dishwashers in the kitchens downstairs.' As well as the waitress uniform she'd used to sneak into the event. 'If once you see it you're not convinced to at least investigate the possibility that Nico is related to you and your brother, I'll never darken your door again. I promise.'

It wasn't exactly much of a bargain. After all, he was about to have her escorted off the premises and thrown in jail. The chances of her ever being able to get within fifty feet of him again were unlikely. But it was the only bargaining chip she had.

She waited for a few pregnant moments. Her heart shrank in her chest when he glanced down at her fingers and she removed her hand from his sleeve. But when he lifted the phone to his ear again her breath clogged her lungs, the desperate bubble of hope expanding in her throat.

Please, God, let Lukas Blackstone give Nico this one chance. And I'll never ask for another miracle again. I promise.

'Tanner,' he said into the phone—his voice seeming to echo from a million miles away as the painful hope began to cut off her air supply. 'Get one of the team to go to the kitchens. There's a bag hidden behind one of the dishwashers. Bring it here.'

The breath that shuddered out made her giddy, the light in the room becoming blinding. 'Thank you.'

He tucked his phone into the inside pocket of his tuxedo jacket.

'I'll give it to you,' he said, his scepticism still plain on his face. 'You're as good an actress as your sister.'

She nodded, suddenly feeling the urge to laugh at the odd note of admiration. But as the hollow chuckle worked its way up her chest, his face—dark and forbidding and unconvinced—seemed to float in front of her. Until all she could see was the scar, pulsing and glowing in the light.

She lifted a finger, which felt like a dead weight attached to the end of her palm—no longer able to control the urge to explore the rough skin.

Her fingertip touched his cheek. His eyes flared, the dark fire burning her from the inside out. But he didn't move as she drew her finger along the jagged line, feeling the warmth of his skin, the flex of the muscle in his jaw. And the pain in her stomach clenched and released, his face melding with Nico's.

'I'm sorry,' she whispered, her heart breaking for him as she imagined him as a boy—like Nico—vulnerable and hurting.

He stiffened and drew away, the flare of irritation turning to something much more dangerous. She dropped her finger, blinking furiously to keep the exhaustion—and that strange foggy feeling of connection—at bay.

What on earth were you thinking?

'Don't touch me again, Miss O'Hara,' he said. 'I can't be swayed by a beautiful woman the way my brother was.'

She collapsed onto the couch as he ordered the two bodyguards who had been outside the door to watch her. But as he left the room one foolish, shameful thought ran through her mind...

Did he just call me beautiful?

The next twenty minutes seemed to last a millennium or two, as Bronte tried to keep alive the vague hope that everything would work out okay when Lukas saw Nikky's photo.

The huge picture window opposite the couch looked out onto the Manhattan night, the room's muted lighting casting a warm glow over the white stucco walls. The exquisite cream and blue silk furnishings were a keynote of the Blackstone brand, expensive and stylish—and yet more evidence of Blackstone's wealth and power, as if she needed it.

Their conversation—and her ignominious exit from the Ball—kept running through her brain, along with the visceral punch of heat. Her head started to ache as a flush of reaction worked its way up to her hairline. The two bodyguards remained by the door, apparently oblivious to her distress. Or maybe they were just being polite.

'Do you think I'll get arrested?' she finally managed, hoping to distract herself with conversation.

'That will be up to Mr Blackstone,' said the older one, not unkindly.

Just as the guard said the words, the door opened and in marched the man himself, sucking all the oxygen out of the room. Bronte pulled herself upright, feeling desperately exposed in her faded ball gown as his gaze raked over her.

The two bodyguards straightened, like soldiers snapping to attention.

'Leave us,' Blackstone said, and they both left with a discreet nod.

Did Blackstone have that effect on all his employees? she wondered as her own heart galloped into her throat.

Blackstone had taken off his tuxedo and the black tie. The rolled-up sleeves of his white dress shirt emphasised the muscular power of his forearms—deeply tanned and furred with dark hair. The waves of hair on his head shone black in the room's lighting and lay in deep grooves as if he'd run his fingers through it, but if he was at all unsettled by their encounter he certainly wasn't showing it. His expression was as intent and controlled as before.

Bronte swallowed. She felt shaky but she had the distinct impression that showing any weakness to this man would be a major mistake.

Her head began to pound, the heat on her cheeks scalding her insides as his gaze travelled over the creased satin dress. Somehow her hair had collapsed—she couldn't even imagine what a wreck she must look like, but she pushed the futile moment of vanity to one side. She didn't have time to care about her appearance, or what he thought of her.

'Have you seen the pictures of Nico?' she asked.

'Yes,' he said.

'You have?' The panic became huge. He still looked unmoved and impassive. How could he not have noticed the resemblance? Between himself and Nico? When it was so clear to her? 'But surely…'

'My medical team have contacted the paediatrician at Westminster Children's Hospital in your phone's contacts,' he cut into her frantic reasoning.

'Then you believe me?' she said, the hope like a sunburst inside her.

But, instead of looking moved, he simply frowned. 'There's enough of a resemblance to require further investigation. That's all.'

It's not a no.

She clung to the lifeline, feeling light-headed again. 'When?' she asked, knowing that time was of the essence. '*When* are you planning to do this further investigation?'

Please let it be soon. Surely he could get tested in New York. That would work. They could feed the results back to the team in the UK, then they'd know if Blackstone was a suitable partial match for the new treatment.

He glanced at his watch. 'We're leaving in twenty minutes, once the helicopter is fuelled.'

'We?' she said, staggered. 'Where are we going?' *And in a helicopter?*

'To JFK,' he said, as if it were obvious. 'The company jet is taking us to London. We should arrive by eight a.m. tomorrow. The hospital is expecting us.'

The leap of joy despite his sharp tone almost choked her. 'Really? You'll get tested straight away then?'

'All I'm prepared to do is a DNA test,' he said flatly. He still didn't sound that convinced, but she didn't care. Because she knew once the DNA results came in the truth would be revealed.

'And when Nico turns out to be Alexei's son?' she asked, her joy hard to contain. Because she knew he wouldn't have a choice then. He would have to get tested, once he knew for sure Nico was his nephew.

She hadn't messed everything up by punching him. Nico still had a chance.

But, instead of saying anything about that, he simply said, 'Then you're going to have some serious questions to answer.'

He stalked out of the room and an assistant arrived with a borrowed coat and her bag. And as she got ready to leave it dawned on Bronte that her battle with Lukas Blackstone was far from over. Because he didn't sound excited or remotely pleased that he might have discovered a long-lost nephew.

He sounded furious. With her. And the whole situation. And more formidable and unforgiving than ever.

CHAPTER TWO

THE HELICOPTER CIRCLED the roof of Westminster Children's Hospital ten hours later. Bronte wrapped her coat around her, still wearing the green satin gown she'd attended the Blackstone Ball in what felt like several lifetimes ago. She had no idea where her tote had ended up and she certainly wasn't about to ask Lukas about it. .

She'd barely spoken to him during the journey. The questions whirling around in her head about Nico in between the fitful sleep she'd managed on the luxury jet all ones she was too scared to ask as they were whisked from JFK to Heathrow.

Not that he'd given her much of an opportunity. He'd ignored her during the journey, working on his laptop and taking a series of calls during the helicopter flight from the hotel in Manhattan and on the flight across the Atlantic.

Bronte had been overawed enough by the whole experience—she'd never travelled in a helicopter before, let alone a private jet—without borrowing more stress by trying to interrogate the man about his intentions towards his soon-to-be nephew. But that hadn't stopped the questions flooding her brain as he ignored her.

She'd stupidly assumed when he told her of the trip that he must be softening. But why should that be the case? Dread edged out the last of the hope in her stomach. What made her think that Lukas would be any better than most men? Her own father had discarded her and her sister when they were almost too young to remember him, walking out one day and simply never coming back.

Their mother had spent years searching for him, convinced he'd been killed in some freak accident, or lost his memory or some such fanciful nonsense, only to discover ten years after he'd disappeared—from a chance article in a local paper—that he'd been living in a neighbouring borough with his new wife.

Bronte huddled in her coat as the crisp morning air slid through the helicopter cabin and the vast black machine's runners touched down on the hospital helipad. The memory of that hideous day still haunted her.

She could still remember the childish anticipation as her mother had dressed her and her sister in their Sunday best clothes and told them they were going to see their daddy. And the dispassionate look on the strange man's face when he answered the door and told her mother he'd moved on. He hadn't even glanced at Bronte and Darcy as they clung to their mother's side.

Her mother had sobbed all the way home on the Tube. And the truth was Ellie O'Hara had never really recovered from that final terrible rejection.

Bronte had made a point of never thinking of her father again. Of trying to erase that day, so she could bury all those gut-wrenching feelings of inadequacy and insecurity that were wrapped up in her only real memory of him. But she couldn't seem to stop herself from replaying it in minute detail ever since she'd boarded Lukas Blackstone's private jet.

Probably because thinking about her father made her think of the only other time in her life when she had been forced to focus all her hopes and dreams on the reaction of a man who had the emotional integrity of a stone.

The problem was, knowing what a bastard Lukas Blackstone was didn't help. Because all it did was make her more aware of exactly how powerless she was.

What would she do if Blackstone refused to help Nico when the blood tie was confirmed? And, really, how good were the chances he would help? She'd had that momentary surge of optimism, but her hope seemed more and more misguided. What evidence did she have that Lukas was even capable of any emotion other than anger and cynicism?

Lukas left the aircraft with the executive assistant. Bronte scrambled after them.

Seeing Dr Patel and her wonderful neighbour Maureen Fitzgerald, who had been visiting Nico at the hospital while she was away, standing at the entrance to the heliport gave her some relief.

She was going to see Nico. After three days away from him in New York, she'd missed him terribly.

'Mr Blackstone, I'm so pleased you have agreed to come,' Dr Patel greeted Lukas with a smile on her face. 'As I told your medical team on the phone, Nico is…'

Lukas held up his hand. 'There's no point in talking to me about the boy until we get the results of the DNA test. Then we can proceed. I believe my legal team have also been in touch.'

Legal team?

'What legal team?' Bronte asked, unable to keep the high note of panic out of her voice. She was jetlagged and exhausted; she needed to see Nico, but she didn't like the way Lukas Blackstone seemed to be taking over. He was in the UK now. He couldn't just order her or the staff around.

Apparently, though, Lukas hadn't got the message because he barely spared her a glance before saying, 'Perhaps you should go and see your nephew. I don't think we require your presence while I take a blood test.'

She wanted to argue, to ask again why his legal team were getting involved in any of this, but as Lukas and his entourage were ushered down the hallway by Dr Patel, Maureen stepped forward to give her a motherly hug.

'Bronte, it's so good to see you. Nico will be overjoyed. He's been asking after you every day. I brought the clothing you texted about.'

'Oh thank you... I can't wait to see him too,' Bronte said, grateful for Maureen's steadfast presence and the chance to change out of the gown. But as she craned her neck, trying to see Lukas's tall frame as he disappeared down the corridor, a terrible feeling of foreboding descended.

'And it's such spectacular news that Mr Blackstone has come over to help,' Maureen added, but the enthusiasm in her voice only made the ball of anxiety in Bronte's stomach knot.

'Is it?' she said.

Maureen's warm smile became quizzical. 'What's wrong, dear? You don't look as ecstatic as I thought you would.'

Bronte sighed. Maureen had been her rock ever since she'd moved into the flat above Bronte's a year ago. A retired nurse with no family of her own, she had been only too willing to step in whenever Bronte needed a babysitter. She'd been indispensable since Nico's illness. And Nico adored her.

'I'm not sure Blackstone has any intention of helping Nico, even if the DNA test comes back positive,' Bronte said, voicing her fears.

Maureen glanced over her shoulder, but her smile remained relaxed. 'Bronte, you're tired. And stressed. You really mustn't worry any more than you have to. Dr Patel told me Mr Blackstone made a million-dollar donation to the hospital's charitable trust last night. And he's come all this way. Surely he wouldn't have done all that if he didn't intend to help Nikky?'

Blackstone had made a million-dollar donation? The news stunned Bronte, but it did nothing to ease her panic, or her sense of foreboding.

Maureen squeezed Bronte's arm. 'All you really have to worry about now is whether Mr Blackstone is the match we need.' The older woman's smile glowed with all the optimism Bronte no longer felt. 'Given that he's the spitting image of Nikky, I think we can already hazard a guess what the DNA test will reveal.'

Bronte nodded, forcing her jetlagged mind not to go to places she couldn't handle right now. 'Okay.'

They walked down the corridor together to the children's ward. Maureen left her at the door with another hug and an admonition not to worry.

But still the anxiety threatened to choke her as she rushed in to see Nico. What if the donation wasn't about generosity, but about control? She didn't trust Lukas Blackstone as far as she could throw him.

And what had he meant by saying *she* would have serious questions to answer?

CHAPTER THREE

ALEXEI HAS A SON. A son who is seriously ill.

Lukas kept his face carefully impassive. But his mind was reeling with shock at the news... And the strange hollow space in his chest was not helping.

So Darcy O'Hara hadn't lied. And neither had her sister. But any charitable feelings he might have felt for the women—particularly Bronte—were quickly quashed. She'd kept the boy's existence a secret for three years. What if the child hadn't gotten sick? Would she ever have told him about his brother's son?

Doubtful.

He remembered the defiance in her eyes and he let the welcome wave of temper consume the black hole in his stomach.

'The DNA results don't just confirm a ninety-nine per cent probability that your brother fathered Nico.' The young doctor smiled. 'They also suggest a very good likelihood of a match between you and Nico for the purposes of his treatment. We'll have to do a proper work-up, which will take approximately twenty-four hours, to check all the specifics but, given that you and his father were identical twins, the chances are you will be a perfect candidate, if you're willing to give your consent?'

'Of course,' he said. If his bone marrow could save the child, he'd have to be a monster not to agree to do it.

Especially as Alexei had always longed for a child. It was the news that he would never father one that had sent Alexei into a tailspin of destructive behaviour as a teenager. While Lukas had stamped out any and all emotions that could make him vulnerable as a child, Alexei had done exactly the opposite—determined to live life on the edge, test every boundary and embrace the recklessness that had eventually killed him. The irony didn't escape Lukas now—the woman he had blamed for his brother's demise had actually given Alexei a life after his death.

For that reason alone, this child must bear the Blackstone name.

'Would you like to meet your nephew?' the doctor asked. 'While we wait for the blood work?'

Lukas felt the hollow sensation grow. He wanted to say no. The one thing he had no desire to do was bond with this child. But he supposed it would be necessary to at least meet the boy.

'Certainly, but I have business to attend to first.' He needed to start putting the wheels in motion—to make sure he controlled this situation from here on.

He stood up and tugged his cell phone out of his pocket. 'I'll come back in later today to meet the child.' Once he was fully prepared for the encounter.

The doctor sent him a tentative smile, obviously confused by his reluctance to meet his nephew immediately, but she didn't comment except to say, 'I'd like to inform Bronte of the news—she'll be overjoyed to hear that you may well be the partial match we need.'

He nodded and then left the room, making the first call to his lawyer.

Somehow he doubted Bronte would be overjoyed for long.

The boy was a Blackstone now—and, once the news got out, even his devoted aunt wouldn't be able to protect the child from the fallout.

'So this is good news?' Bronte felt something break open inside her as Dr Patel smiled benevolently and nodded.

'It's excellent news, Bronte. Obviously we have to do a full work-up, but already the signs are phenomenally good.'

'And Blackstone has agreed to donate his bone marrow?' Bronte asked, the joy starting to roll through her, smashing through all the barriers, all the walls she had constructed against the worst of her fears for so long. She'd had to stay strong for Nico, had refused to admit defeat or to shed a single tear through the long hours of treatment. So much so that this new glimmer of hope felt like a massive relief.

'Yes, he has,' the doctor repeated, not for the first time.

'Did you tell him how gruelling it is?' Bronte asked again, not quite able to believe Lukas Blackstone was the saviour she'd hoped for.

'Yes, as I said, I've talked him through the procedure and he didn't even bat an eyelid before agreeing.'

Bronte's knees began to shake, the exhaustion rising up to smash through the numbness. She felt as if she were floating—floating on a wave of hope—as a single tear rolled down her cheek.

'Bronte, sit down.' The doctor sounded firm as she pressed her into one of the hard plastic chairs in the children's ward waiting room. Then she handed her a tissue.

Bronte blew her nose loudly and wiped the foolish tear away, trying to take it all in. A laugh, the first real laugh she'd managed in longer than she could remember, burst out. 'I can't… It's such good news I can't quite believe it.'

Dr Patel sat down beside her and patted her arm. 'Obviously we've still got a long way to go, but all the signs are good now and in our favour.'

'I know… It's just…' She turned to Dr Patel. 'I thought he was such a jerk. I'd convinced myself even if he were Nico's uncle he'd refuse to help him.' She screwed up the tissue in her hands, suddenly feeling guilty about her doubts and desperately ashamed of her behaviour.

She'd judged Lukas Blackstone without knowing him, had assumed he was an arrogant, privileged, entitled jerk. And now he'd agreed to do something totally amazing, and not inconsiderable, for a child he didn't even know. The guy was a hero, whatever way you looked at it.

She sniffed, letting hope seep into her soul and forcing herself to acknowledge the truth.

Why not admit it? She hadn't just been conflicted about alerting Lukas to Nico's existence because it would mean breaking her promise to Darcy. But because for so long she'd been Nico's only relative. And while she'd been desperate to find a donor for him, a small, insecure little part of her heart had wanted Nico's saviour to be her.

She stood. There was no time for tears now either, or recriminations. She needed to speak to Lukas, to thank him for all he was doing, and for all he'd agreed to do, the way she hadn't done properly when he'd agreed to fly his private jet over the Atlantic just to substantiate her claims.

Yup, that was a pretty big clue right there that he wasn't a total jerk, Bronte, you dope.

She almost winced at the ungrateful way she'd behaved on the flight over, resenting his presence and creating all sorts of nightmare scenarios and ulterior motives while ignoring the obvious answer—that Lukas Blackstone had wanted to help the boy who might be his nephew.

She let out a deep breath as she followed Dr Patel back onto Harry Potter Ward.

Lukas Blackstone was Nico's uncle. It was official now. And she was going to have to get over any and all irrational fears about letting Lukas into Nico's life. Because, of course, Lukas would want to get to know his brother's child. He would want to play a part in his life. It was highly likely that the billionaire was going to be responsible for saving her baby boy's life—which gave him certain rights. Lots of rights.

Nico sent her a sleepy grin as Bronte walked to his bedside.

'You're awake, Nikky!' she said, grinning at him as she stroked the short silky curls of hair that had started to grow back after the latest round of chemo.

Her heart juddered. Maybe it would even be his last round of chemo.

'I know,' he said and she laughed.

He stretched out his arms and yawned. And she gathered him into her arms to hug him. 'How are you feeling?'

His breath felt warm against her cheek as he snuggled into her embrace. 'I'm tired,' he said.

'Okay, but I've got some important news for you. Maybe I should wait till tomorrow to tell you. I don't want you to fall asleep.'

He pushed out of her arms and his little face screwed up in a frown of disgust, which only made her smile more. The resemblance to Lukas Blackstone was stunning, especially when Nico looked grumpy, she thought, stupidly tickled by the observation.

'I'm not going to fall asleep,' Nico said. 'I'm not a

baby. I'm going to be three and three-quarters next week.' He yawned again, contradicting his assertion somewhat. 'What's the 'portant news?' Nico asked dreamily.

'There's someone who has come all the way from New York to meet you. Which is a long way away, across an ocean. Remember I told you I was going to look for him, when I had to leave you?'

She'd made her trip into a story—a story which she had been careful not to imbue with too much hope—but it was hard to contain her optimism now.

'The man with the special bones? Who's going to make me better?' Nico's head lifted. The sparkle of excitement was something she hadn't seen for a long time in Nico's brown eyes and she realised that however non-committal she had tried to be, however careful, and however hard she'd tried not to hope too much, Nico had hoped for both of them. 'Did you find him?' he asked.

'Yes, I did. Remember I told you he's your daddy's brother?'

'My daddy that's dead?'

'That's right. Lukas is a very special brother to your daddy called an identical twin, and he's come all this way to meet you, and hopefully to help you get better.' If the treatment didn't work she would deal with it, but right now she wanted to feed the glow in Nico's eyes. Whatever else Lukas Blackstone did, she would always be grateful to him for giving Nico hope.

Her eyes stung again when Nico's lips crinkled into the cheeky smile she'd missed so much. 'Is he a super-hero?'

'Yes, he is. He's your own personal superhero—that's pretty cool, isn't it?'

'Is that the Superman?' Nico pointed over her shoulder. 'He's super-big.'

Bronte glanced over her shoulder. The blood rushed to her cheeks. And pounded hard in her chest. Despite the deliberately bright and airy surroundings of Harry Potter Ward, Lukas Blackstone looked as austere and forbidding as ever as he approached the bed with two men in dark suits and a woman in high heels holding a smartphone and busily typing things into it.

Keeping her hand securely on Nico's narrow shoulder, Bronte got off the bed to face him, disconcerted by the huge height disadvantage. She knew she wasn't a tall woman, but did he have to be quite so enormous?

'Hi, Lukas, we're so happy to see you,' she said, trying to put as much friendliness and warmth into her voice as she could for Nico's sake. If she found the man intimidating, how would a three-and-three-quarter-year-old feel?

'Are you?' Lukas said, the cynical lift of his eyebrow making her feel unbearably self-conscious before his gaze transferred to the child.

'Yes, absolutely,' she lied, wanting desperately to mean it. Clasping Nico's hand, she was about to introduce them when Nico—who was clearly much braver than her—pushed up in the bed.

'I'm Nico,' he said. 'Auntie Bronte says you're my superhero. And you're going to make me better.'

Lukas glanced her way before saying to the boy, his voice even gruffer than usual, 'I'm going to try.'

With a burst of energy that reminded Bronte poignantly of the little boy he had been, Nico leapt forward and scrambled across the bed to wrap his arms as far as he could around Lukas's waist and bury his head in his shirt front. 'Thank you, thank you, thank you!' the little boy declared. 'I hate being sick—it's horrid.'

And then he began to cry, deep heart-wrenching sobs that tore at Bronte's chest as she gripped his shoulders, trying to soothe him, desperate to draw him away from Lukas, who had tensed and lifted his hands—looking for a split second both shocked and wary...and completely lost for words.

Clearly the big bad billionaire had zero experience with kids.

The situation would almost be comical if Bronte hadn't been feeling so over-emotional herself. Scooping Nico up, she placed him back in the bed and tucked him under the covers, careful not to put any more strain on the line in his arm.

Ignoring Lukas, who was still standing stiffly by the bed, she smoothed Nico's hair back from his forehead as the boy bit back the sobs which he must have been keeping in for a long time. 'It's all right, Nikky. Cry as much as you want.'

He hiccupped slightly, the tears passing. 'But I don't want to cry. I want to be a brave boy.'

'You are a brave boy,' she whispered against his face and gave him a little squeeze, making him smile through the last remnants of his tears. 'Even if you cry, remember?'

He nodded but his eyelids were already drooping, the brief spurt of action having exhausted his frail stamina. 'Can the superman stay with me?'

Bronte glanced over her shoulder to see Lukas still looking shocked and wary. 'Of course he can. He'll stay until you fall asleep, okay?'

Lukas gave a terse nod.

''kay,' Nico murmured, apparently soothed by Lukas's austere presence. This child wasn't just brave; he was heroic. But he was still just a little boy—a little boy who had been forced to deal with far too much already. A little boy who desperately needed her to be the brave one right now. As if to confirm the thought, Nico stuffed a thumb into his mouth and gripped a chunk of her hair in his small fist, the way he had done ever since he was a baby. 'Sing me *Puff*,' he said.

She sang his favourite nursery song about a magic dragon, imbuing the notes with all the love she felt and the new sense of hope, until he fell asleep.

Snuggling against him, she breathed in his scent. Even tinged with the chemical scent of the hospital ward, it still gave her the essential rush of love she'd felt the first time she'd held his tiny body in her arms.

'You'll be better soon, Nico. I promise,' she whispered.

Kissing his cheek, she got off the bed, her weariness buoyed by a new wave of possibility. But when she caught sight of Lukas Blackstone, still standing by the bed staring down at Nico, she felt a jolt of panic and even fear.

No matter what happened now, their lives would be irrevocably changed, having this man in them. And right now she'd never felt less ready to deal with that change. And him.

She straightened as his gaze moved from the bed and locked on her—the jolt became hot and fluid, disconcerting her. He studied her with that cool dark gaze and she struggled to contain her response. Her visceral physical reaction to this man was something she needed to control—not least because it made no sense. And it would only make this situation more difficult.

'He's so small,' he murmured, surprising her.

'Actually, Nico is tall for his age,' she replied. 'Despite his illness.'

Probably because he's related to you, she thought, having to crane her neck to address him. Her gaze took in those broad shoulders and the tall, lean, intimidating frame. Even with his jacket off and his shirt sleeves rolled up he seemed forbidding—she tried and failed to imagine Nico as a young man. Would he be that tall? That handsome?

The scar on Lukas's cheek tensed as he returned his gaze to the bed and the child sleeping peacefully on it.

He studied Nico for a long time, clearly taking in every aspect of the child, but his features registered little or no emotion.

One thing Nico wouldn't be, Bronte silently promised herself, was so arrogant and cynical—so devoid of warmth. She wondered again what had happened to him to make him so determined to keep his feelings so closely guarded. Because something must have happened. However imperturbable he seemed, she had seen the shocked emotion cross his face when Nico had hugged him, making her sure he had feelings—he just didn't want to reveal them.

'Why did you tell him I was going to save him?' he said at last. 'There's no guarantee that I will be a suitable match and, even if I am, this is an experimental treatment.' There was no censure in the question, the tone pragmatic, but still Bronte felt the flicker of criticism, the need to defend herself. She bit back the caustic response though, as she spotted the plaster on the inside of his arm, covering the small bruise forming where the doctor had taken his blood for testing.

Lukas Blackstone was here—and prepared to do the right thing—for that she would give him as much encouragement and cooperation as she possibly could. It was also pretty obvious he had absolutely no knowledge of kids, which gave her the upper hand. Not that they were in competition. But she could guide him, if she handled the situation sensibly—instead of going in with all her insecurities blazing. The dull red mark on his chin made her feel ashamed of her previous interactions with him.

'Right now, what Nico needs is hope,' she replied. 'And while it's an experimental treatment, they've had terrific results so far. The doctor also said already that the blood work suggests you'll be a near perfect match.'

'Okay,' he said. 'But in the future could I suggest you don't mythologise me too much. I'm unlikely to have much interaction with the boy once this is over.'

'You won't?' she blurted out, forgetting that having him in their lives wasn't something she particularly wanted. 'But you're his uncle.'

'I realise that,' he said, the flicker of acknowledgement oddly gratifying. 'But I'm not particularly good with children.'

She had gathered that much already but, before she could point out that he could learn, the way she had, he added, 'And I have no aptitude or desire to learn.'

The statement was so unequivocal she felt desperately sorry for him. But instead of saying the first thing that came into her head—that Nico had already made an attachment to him, and that his life would be so much richer with this little boy in it—she stopped herself. It wasn't her job to tell this man what his relationship with his nephew should or could be. And she'd certainly be much better off not having to deal with him on a regular basis.

'Okay,' she murmured. 'If that's what you want.'

'Mr Blackstone, the sale on the property you selected is complete,' the woman standing next to him, who had been tapping on her smartphone throughout their conversation, piped up.

Blackstone nodded. 'Good work, Lisa.'

'Not that good, Mr Blackstone,' Lisa said, still clicking. 'I'm afraid they wouldn't settle for anything less than twenty-eight point five.'

Twenty-eight point five what? Bronte thought, wondering why Blackstone was making property deals in the midst of a children's hospital. Wasn't that taking multitasking a bit too far?

'Not a problem,' Lukas replied. 'Twenty-eight point five million sterling isn't bad for a house in that location.'

Bronte simply blinked, feeling as if she'd just jumped back into the alternate reality she'd been ushered into twelve hours ago when she'd found herself aboard Lukas Blackstone's private jet climbing into the night sky over JFK.

Twenty-eight point five million pounds? What kind of house was he buying?

It didn't take her long to find out when he continued talking to Lisa, who Bronte had realised must be another of his many personal assistants.

'Arrange to move Ms O'Hara and the boy's possessions in as soon as possible. Hire the staff. And then handle the other details.'

'Excuse me, but where is Ms O'Hara moving to?' Bronte asked. 'And what staff?'

'I've purchased you and Nico a property in Regent's Park,' Lukas said with about as much inflection as if he'd just informed her he'd bought her a caramel latte. 'Lisa is my executive assistant in the London office of Blackstone's,' he continued. 'She'll make all the necessary arrangements to see you settled in there tonight. Hire the necessary staff. So it's ready for the boy when he's well enough to leave the hospital.'

'But we already have a home in Hackney,' Bronte said. Maybe their tiny basement flat wasn't exactly salubrious but it was all she could afford on her salary.

'It's no longer suitable,' he said, as if that answered anything.

'Why not?' she replied, trying to stay calm and stop the panic from fuelling her temper. Maybe she should be grateful for his generosity but what gave him the right to swoop in and take over their lives?

Instead of giving her an answer, he spoke to the two men in dark suits who had accompanied him onto the ward and remained silent and watchful throughout the conversation. 'This is Nico, gentlemen.' He indicated the boy. 'He's a Blackstone. I expect him to be guarded with your lives. There is never to be less than two guards on him at all times. Understood?'

Both men nodded.

'Wait a minute.' Bronte grasped Lukas's arm, immediately withdrawing her touch when he swung round to trap her in that dark gaze. 'Who are these men?' she asked. 'I don't know them from Adam, and neither does Nico. I haven't agreed to them guarding him,' Bronte finished, her voice rising despite her best efforts to remain calm.

'My team have already cleared their presence here with the consultant and the ward staff. They're part of a six-man team of bodyguards who will be guarding my nephew from now on.'

My nephew? So what does that make me?

'Well, I haven't agreed to their presence and he was my nephew first,' she hissed, hating Lukas Blackstone for making her sound ridiculous. Nico's welfare wasn't something to have a catfight over, but she wasn't about to have her and Nico's life disrupted by this man's arrogant decision to take charge after spending exactly ten minutes at Nico's bedside.

Instead of replying, Lukas closed strong fingers round

her upper arm and led her towards the exit. 'Let's take this outside before we wake any of the patients.'

His grip wasn't painful, but it was so firm and unyielding she had no choice but to keep pace with his long strides as he led her out of the ward and into an empty waiting room like an unruly child. The zip and zing of sensation shooting up her arm only added to the galling feeling of impotence and the wave of temper which was fast becoming unstoppable.

'Get the ball rolling on the relocation, Lisa.' He spoke to the assistant, who trotted along beside them both—the two of them ignoring Bronte's struggles to free herself from his unyielding grip. 'I want it completed as soon as we leave here tonight. And then arrange my nephew's move to the private hospital in Chelsea for tomorrow morning.'

The personal assistant bowed—as if he were some sort of feudal lord—then scurried off, leaving them alone in the waiting room.

As he closed the door, Bronte yanked her arm free and scrambled back. Rubbing her biceps where his touch still burned, she tried to gather her wits about her, and stop the renewed wave of panic from consuming her temper.

She'd wanted to be grateful, to be helpful, to let him know how much his contribution, his willingness to help Nico in his hour of need meant to them both. But this didn't feel helpful: it felt overwhelming. And oppressive. And controlling.

She hated this feeling of powerlessness. Because it reminded her of the little girl she'd once been with an absent father and a mother who couldn't cope. But she had to stand her ground, to state her case, no matter how intimidated or overwhelmed she felt.

Lukas Blackstone was clearly a man used to having

his every order and command obeyed without question. But she was Nico's sole carer, the person who had always had his best interests at heart.

Lukas had just said he wanted no real part in his own nephew's life—which also made her the only one in this room who loved Nico and would continue to love him and care for him long after Lukas's involvement in saving his life was over. That gave her some rights. Rights that he seemed intent on taking away.

'Nico's not transferring to a private hospital,' she said, as succinctly as she could while her whole body was shaking with reaction. 'Any more than we're both moving into a twenty-eight-point-five-million-pound house in Regent's Park.'

His brows flattened, the dark eyes becoming stormy as the scar on his cheek twitched in warning.

'I appreciate your generosity, but it's not necessary,' she continued, feeling as if she were trying to placate a rampaging lion with a feather duster. 'Nico's treatment team is here. His home is our flat. And Nico's my responsibility. I'm his guardian and I decide what's best for him. Not you.'

The surge of adrenaline hit Lukas unawares, and shot straight into his crotch. He braced himself against the spike of temper that swiftly followed.

So his perverse reaction to this woman hadn't been an aberration. Something about her had the power to turn him on, even when she was daring to defy him. Especially when she was daring to defy him, he realised, taking in the sheen of enraged moisture turning her eyes into deep emerald pools.

The rise and fall of her breathing made her full breasts press against the simple tank top she'd donned after their flight over the Atlantic. The flight when he'd buried himself in work and details to ignore her dozing in the bed at the back of the cabin.

Unfortunately, it hadn't worked.

His unprecedented reaction to the boy a few minutes ago had only confused things further. Seeing the child in the flesh for the first time had been a shock. A shock he'd thought he'd been prepared for but hadn't. The hazy childhood memories had slammed into him before he'd had a chance to completely mask his reaction. Having the child's arms cling to him, seeing the curls of dark hair, so like his brother's at that age, feeling sobs racking the child's small frame had been a torture he had not been prepared for—leaving him feeling raw and exposed.

And now this ludicrous sexual reaction to Bronte O'Hara's childish show of defiance, which he also seemed powerless to control, was the last straw.

'Nico is a Blackstone,' he said tightly, keeping a rein on his temper and the desire to yank her into his arms and feast on that mouth until neither of them could think straight.

'I know he is. I came all the way to Manhattan to tell you that, remember. But I don't see what that has to…'

'You announced it in public at the Full Moon Ball in front of about a hundred journalists and social media bloggers,' he continued, clinging on to his patience with an effort when she still looked clueless. 'Those same journalists and bloggers will be well aware that my jet left JFK with you and me on board less than an hour later.'

'I still don't see how…'

'Speculation is already rife on the Internet. By tomorrow morning, Nico's illness, his whereabouts, your whereabouts, the location of your apartment and every other minute detail of your life, your sister's life and death, and her one-night stand with Alexei will be all over the gossip columns and the Internet. Blackstone's main offices here and in Manhattan have already been besieged with requests for a comment. The Blackstone fortune is worth upwards of thirty billion dollars at a conservative estimate.'

Her deep green eyes popped wide. 'You're joking!'

The sprinkle of freckles across her nose brightened as her skin flushed a vibrant shade of red to match her hair. Apropos of exactly nothing, it occurred to him that he couldn't remember the last time he'd seen a grown woman blush—and certainly not with the spontaneity and regularity of Bronte O'Hara. Why he should find it captivating he had no idea. Maybe it was simply because it made her so easy to read.

'I'm not joking,' he said, but strangely he felt like smiling. She didn't look defiant any more or argumentative—she looked horrified. 'And the moment Dr Patel told me the results of the DNA test, Nico became my heir—which means he's now worth upwards of thirty billion dollars too.'

'But we don't need your money. We just need your stem cells and your bone marrow.' The blush intensified as he watched her realise what she'd just said. 'I'm sorry. I didn't mean that to sound so mercenary.'

If she didn't know it sounded exactly the opposite of mercenary, who was he to enlighten her?

'But seriously, a twenty-eight-and-a-half-million-pound house?' she continued. 'I can't accept it. It's too much.'

'It's not for you. It's for Nico,' he said, even though he realised that for the boy's sake she would need to live there just as much, which would allow him to keep a close eye on her.

The blood pounded back into his groin at the proprietorial thought and he had to steel himself against the urge to drag her back into his arms and kiss her senseless again.

He was not making any moves on this woman.

'And it's really not your place to deny him his birthright,' he finished. 'As Alexei's son, he deserves Alexei's share of the fortune.'

Lukas could only hope that Nico didn't inherit any more of the Blackstone curse. But that seemed unlikely. From the brief interaction he'd witnessed between Bronte and the child, she was a devoted mother to the boy in everything but name.

His own mother had had no interest in him or Alexei once they'd been born—happily handing over their care to a string of nannies and governesses so she could spend as much of their father's fortune as was humanly possible before her untimely death in a light aircraft crash a few days before their fifth birthdays.

He could still remember the nanny informing them of the news—and both him and Alexei wondering why the usually stern woman had looked so upset.

He hadn't felt the loss then and he still didn't now. He had cut off the need to be nurtured as a child. Had forced himself to become emotionally self-sufficient and he considered that a strength. Because he knew how weak it could make you when those needs weren't met. But, even so, he was glad Alexei's son wasn't having to struggle through this difficult time in his life alone.

'But he's just a little boy, and he's dealing with so much already,' Bronte pleaded. Noticing the dark bruises under her eyes—not for the first time—Lukas acknowledged it wasn't just the boy who had been through the wars of late. She looked exhausted. And while he still felt a certain anger towards her—because she'd kept the boy's existence a secret—he had to give her credit for doing it for the right reasons. Unfortunately, rightly or wrongly, Nico was now in the eye of the hurricane, which meant he needed protection—something Bronte couldn't possibly understand or provide. He, on the other hand, knew only too well how vulnerable the boy was.

The scar throbbed, the brutal reminder of the ripping pain threatening to surface. He shoved it back.

This is not about you. This is about Alexei's son.

While he had no desire to have a relationship with the boy, the necessary protection was something he could and would provide, whether Bronte liked it or not.

'Couldn't we just pretend he's not your heir?' she added. 'Tell the press a story? I don't want his life disrupted even more.'

'It's too late for that—the story's already out,' he said, astonished at her naïveté. 'My PR people have arranged for me to give a press conference tomorrow to try and contain it. The statement will be brief. I'll announce Nico as my heir, give details of his illness and then request privacy at this difficult time.'

'Will that work?' Bronte asked, the desperate hope in her eyes making him think of a puppy who was used to being kicked but still believed things would work out okay.

He almost felt bad telling her the truth. 'It'll keep the more reputable journalists at bay and should help to deaden the story faster. Cold hard facts never sell as well as lurid speculation. But you still won't be able to return to your apartment, or your former life. Because the press aren't the only threat,' he finished, choosing not to elaborate. She might be young and naïve, but she had been alone with a young child surviving on her wits for

four years; she had to know the depths of depravity some
people would go to when it came to money.

'I see,' she said, sounding dejected, and he could see
she did know. 'I'm sorry for complaining. You're just
trying to do the right thing, and I'm making things more
difficult. But it just all feels so overwhelming.'

Her honesty floored him a little.

'Surely it can't be that tough knowing you'll never
have to scrub another john?' he said, the desire to lift
some of the heavy burden she seemed to be carrying as
unprecedented as his reaction to her.

Her eyes flickered with surprise, then suspicion.
Clearly she hadn't expected him to have her investigated.
Yet more evidence of her naïveté—which he was start-
ing to find far too appealing.

She drew herself up to her full height and stuck out
that stubborn chin. 'There's nothing wrong with scrubbing toilets!' she announced, looking like a pint-sized
Valkyrie. 'Someone has to do it and it's honest work.
You probably pay someone to scrub yours.'

'No doubt,' he said. 'But, whoever they are, I'm sure
they would rather be doing something else, if they could.'

The fact that she had been working so hard, in such a
menial job, when she seemed to be an intelligent and re-
sourceful woman struck him again as above and beyond
the call of duty for an aunt. According to the interim report he'd received from his security team, she'd taken
over the care of her nephew—*their* nephew—when she
was only eighteen, and had worked like a dog in a series
of dead-end jobs to make ends meet. She should have
contacted him about Nico long before now. But the fact
that she hadn't seemed like an act of selflessness now.
And a surprising one at that. She could have used the
child as a bargaining chip and she hadn't.

'I suppose,' she said, but her shoulders slumped and she looked more dejected than ever. 'I'll be honest it's not the john-scrubbing I'll miss, but the anonymity. I guess I didn't really think this through. All I cared about when I came to Manhattan to confront you was making Nico better. I wish I hadn't blurted out the truth in front of all those people. This is all my fault.'

Unable to resist the urge to touch her a moment longer, he tucked a knuckle under her chin and lifted that bright emerald gaze to his.

'It's not your fault. Once Nico's relationship to Alexei was confirmed, the press would have gotten hold of the story eventually.'

'But you've been calm and practical and I've been a basket case.'

Only because he wasn't as emotionally invested in the outcome, he thought dispassionately. But the urge to comfort her and take the regret out of her eyes wouldn't abate.

'This is a difficult situation for both of us,' he said, surprising himself with the desire to meet her honesty with at least some of his own. 'I hadn't expected to become an uncle out of the blue, or to discover at the exact same moment that I may be my nephew's only chance of survival.'

Her head tilted back, dislodging his finger, but the sheen of moisture in her eyes announced the depth of her feelings, and her vulnerability. She really was an open book.

'You're right—of course you're right,' she said and, even though he could hear the strain in her voice, the apology a shot to what he suspected was a phenomenal amount of pride, he could also tell she meant it. 'I haven't given enough thought to what you're going through,' she added. 'I'll try to be more cooperative. And I really do appreciate everything you're doing. You've been amazing and I've been rude.'

The forthright statement made him feel like a fraud—he wasn't going through that much. After all, he barely knew the boy, and he'd never truly grieved for Alexei. As adults they hadn't been that close because he'd never been able to get that close to anyone, not since... He cut off the thought and tucked his hands into his pockets to resist the urge to touch her again.

'So you'll move into the house in Regent's Park without an argument?' He forced himself to make it sound like a question instead of a demand.

He could see the momentary struggle she waged before she nodded. 'Yes. If you're sure it's necessary.'

'It is. And the bodyguards? I need your complete co-operation there too, for Nico's safety.'

'Absolutely. I understand,' she said, but he could see the new struggle. She'd been doing this on her own for so long, he supposed she was finding it hard to let go of control. He tried not to gloat. 'But would it be okay if they wore something more casual?' she added. 'And made an effort not to be too intimidating? Nico's a very sociable kid when he's well, but he's been through a lot recently and he's fragile. I don't want their presence to freak him out.'

'Of course.' Lukas nodded, realising her show of defiance had only been because she was putting the boy's needs first. Needs that would never even have occurred to him. 'I will speak to my security people, tell them to employ men and women who have experience guarding children and know how to relate to them.'

'Thank you.' Again her gratitude seemed heartfelt. 'Could I say something else?' she said, her stubborn chin firming up again.

'Go ahead.'

'I don't want Nico moved to a private hospital.'

He quelled his immediate instinct to shoot down her request. He must force himself to negotiate—not something he had a lot of experience with. But then, when was the last time he had been faced with a woman—or anyone really—who was prepared to refuse him?

'The security in a public hospital isn't strong enough,' he said.

'Then hire more bodyguards, or figure out a way to make it more secure…'

'There's no need to…'

'This hospital is the leading centre in its field on the experimental treatment they're advocating for Nico,' she cut in, jumping on his slight hesitation. 'Without these doctors and this staff, Nico wouldn't even have this chance. Not only that, but he has friends here, among the other patients and the nurses and doctors. It may be a public hospital but it's where Nico needs to be to get well.'

She wasn't asking him, he realised, she was telling him, but the passion in her voice and the vibrant colour in her cheeks told him Nico's welfare was driving her determination and he found he couldn't bring himself to push back. He would get expert independent medical advice to ensure all she was telling him was true—but it was already clear she believed in this place. And maybe that was enough, for now.

For the first time in a long time he found himself forced to back down. 'All right, we'll play it your way for now. You know the boy best.'

'Thank you,' she said again, but the slight edge to her voice suggested she wasn't feeling all that grateful this time. 'And about the staff…'

'The staff are non-negotiable.' This was one issue he

would not be backing down on, he decided as he registered the dark smudges under her eyes again.

'But I really don't think I need staff,' she said. 'I'm perfectly capable of looking after Nico and myself on my own,' she added, the edge in her voice annoying him—almost as much as the strange pressure in his chest at the evidence of her exhaustion.

'Well, you won't be doing that any more. You'll need a chauffeur, a gardener, cleaning staff and a nanny at the very least.' She was being stubborn now. And he was not about to allow her to make herself ill because of some ludicrous sense of misplaced pride.

'Why would I need a chauffeur?' she said. 'I don't even have a car. And I don't need a nanny either. I can look after Nico myself, especially if I won't be able to go back to scrubbing johns,' she said, but her rising frustration had the opposite effect on him as it occurred to him that her determination not to need him, or anything his money could provide, made her the opposite of the gold-digger he'd originally taken her for.

Why that should matter, he had no idea, but it seemed that it did.

'You'll need secure transportation to and from the hospital. Hence the chauffeur.' And the three bullet-proof cars he would be supplying them with, but he didn't see the need to mention that just yet and inflame the situation further. 'And the nanny is simply for backup,' he added, not quite sure why he was so determined to provide one. Maybe it was those damn dark smudges again. He didn't like the idea of her having to struggle on alone—the way she'd struggled so much already.

His nephew's well-being was all that mattered to him. Not hers. But, even so, he felt oddly relieved when he saw the last of the fight go out of her.

'Okay, but I still don't want to employ a stranger. Maybe I could ask Maureen if she'd like to move in with us?'

'Who's Maureen?'

'You met her.' She frowned, clearly unimpressed that he hadn't remembered the woman. 'When you arrived. She's my next door neighbour and she's fabulous with Nico.'

'Is she trained?' he asked.

'She's a retired nurse,' she replied flatly, the green fire of indignation making her eyes sparkle.

So not trained in childcare then. He held back the retort as a lungful of her scent—fresh and beguiling—invaded his senses.

He nodded. 'Okay, I'll instruct Lisa to ensure the housekeeper's quarters are made ready for her. And arrange a suitable salary.' He needed to end this conversation now. He'd spent enough time sparring with this woman over unnecessary details. Details that really shouldn't matter to him this much.

Bronte opened her mouth, as if she were going to disagree with him, but then closed it again. Tension rippled through her small frame. And he knew she felt it too, that visceral tug of yearning.

'I should go back to the ward,' she said, glancing at the door and tucking her hands into the back pockets of her jeans.

The movement made her breasts stretch the cotton tank top she wore, making him aware of the vague outline of her nipples against the worn fabric. He watched them harden into bullets, as the urge to peel down her top and lick the turgid tips lodged in his brain and would not be dislodged.

A bright flush rose on her cheeks, their awkward truce

sharpening on the knife-edge of desire, as the peaks engorged and her lust-blown pupils flooded the deep mossy green of her irises.

What the hell?

She took a cautious step back, the awareness in her expression tempered by wariness. And he noticed the fatigue again, making her eyes look huge in her pale face.

Not the time or the place to deal with this, Blackstone.

'Nico should wake up again in a few hours and I want to be there when he does,' she said, the words rapid, her breathing coarse and uneven.

Was she scared of him, or just of the strength of the sexual chemistry between them?

She lifted a hand out of her pocket and jerked her thumb over her shoulder as she retreated towards the door. 'Would you like to come and sit with me? I'm sure Nico would love to meet you properly when he wakes up.'

He shook his head, and he saw her visibly wilt with relief at his refusal.

'I don't think that will be necessary,' he said, determined to keep that boundary in place. He was more than invested enough in this situation already. He needed to take stock, to properly define the parameters of his interaction, and not just with the boy, apparently, but also with his far too captivating aunt, before he spent any more time with them.

If he spent any time with them, he corrected himself.

'I'll be staying at the Blackstone Park Lane while I'm in London,' he said before she could bolt out of the door. 'Lisa will escort you to your new home when you're finished here. You can let her know if there's anything else you or Nico needs.'

She bobbed her head, her hand trembling on the door

knob. 'Okay, and thanks again.' Her face softened, the emotion shining in her eyes only making her more attractive. And him more tense. 'For coming here, and giving Nico this chance. I know you don't want to be a superhero, but if this works you will be, to me.'

He nodded, not trusting himself to reply, and not understanding the tight feeling in his chest as she left the room.

He wasn't a superhero. He wasn't even a good person. Something she would discover soon enough if they ever decided to act on the sexual chemistry that had flared between them without warning.

Not gonna happen.

He pulled his cell phone out of his pocket and contacted Lisa to set up the press conference for tomorrow. Then he headed out of the waiting room behind Bronte and turned in the opposite direction, walking towards the hospital exit—while attempting to ignore the pulsing ache in his crotch and the tight feeling in his chest which had refused to subside ever since he'd first spotted her at the Ball.

Six hours later, Bronte lay in a huge four-poster bed in a bedroom suite bigger than her whole flat. She stared at the intricate cornicing on the ceiling while she attempted to regulate her breathing and process everything that had happened to her—and Nico—in the last twenty-four hours.

The detached Georgian house—correction, the detached Georgian *palace*—Lukas Blackstone had insisted on buying for her and Nico was as overwhelming as she had expected it to be. Four storeys of ornate stucco painted in pristine white with manicured lawns that led to a wrought iron gate leading onto Regent's Park. But it wasn't this house—correction, palace—that was making her hyperventilate. It was him.

Her breathing sped up again, the heavy thud of her heartbeat squeezing the air out of her lungs.

What was the matter with her? She should be ecstatic about everything. This mansion, the staff, the decision to employ Maureen, who was moving into the housekeeper's cottage tomorrow, Lukas's agreement to donate bone marrow to help find Nikky a cure. But instead she felt completely overwhelmed.

This isn't about Lukas Blackstone. This is about you. And your inexplicable reaction to him.

She sighed. There, she'd admitted it.

The man was just so overpowering. And it wasn't just his vast wealth—which had been shocking enough—but everything about him. His tall muscular body, the harshly masculine face and that compelling scar, that enticing juniper scent, the indomitable presence, the way he seemed intent on bending her to his will and, worst of all, the flash of…something…in his eyes when they'd been in the waiting room together and she'd felt her breasts swell and her nipples tighten under that intense gaze. All she'd wanted in that moment was for him to rip open her T-shirt, drag down her bra, release her heavy breasts from their confinement and feast on them, the way he'd feasted on her mouth the night before at the Ball. She'd gone into some weird erotic trance, which even now felt so vivid and so volatile it shocked her to her core.

She squeezed her thighs together, brutally ashamed of the liquid tug in her abdomen that hadn't gone away since their encounter. Slotting herself into a life totally alien to everything she had ever known seemed like small potatoes compared to having to deal with this uncontrollable, all-consuming hunger.

So there's that.

She placed her arm over her face.

Had he known? What her body had been begging for him to do? Mortification engulfed her, but the burning flush was soon doused by a cold, hard dose of reality.

Oh, please. Why does it even matter if he knew? He would never, ever act on it. Lukas Blackstone dates supermodels and A-list actresses—he's not interested in you. And, even if he were, sex isn't even on your radar. You've got less experience than Snow White for a very good reason. Nico is all that matters at the moment. All that has ever mattered.

And, even if he wasn't, Lukas Blackstone was not someone she would ever consider dating, if she did date. Which she didn't. The women in her family had a bad habit of becoming emotionally besieged by overpowering and emotionally unavailable men. Her mum had done it and so had Darcy. She was not about to follow suit just because of a ridiculous physical reaction which had probably been brought on by fatigue and all her recent emotional upheavals.

Giving in to that split-second urge to jump Lukas Blackstone was not who she was. She was better than that, stronger than that.

She climbed under the ten thousand thread-count sheets, trying to switch her mind off the subject of Lukas and back on to the much more important business of Nico and the weeks ahead. She should be focused on tomorrow and the results of Lukas's blood tests. The operation that would hopefully follow and Nikky's recovery. Lukas Blackstone and that daft little frisson between them was just a distraction.

But even worse, she realised, had been that even more idiotic moment when he'd insisted on hiring a nanny for her, and she'd actually believed—for a second—that he cared about her welfare as well as Nikky's.

Why would he? And why would you even want him to?

She breathed in the scent of freshly laundered linen and new paint as her gaze roamed over the immaculately furnished room, and found the open door to the adjoining suite.

She spotted the corner of Nikky's bed—the bed he would be sleeping in soon, if the treatment worked. Her breathing evened out. At least a little.

Just keep your eyes on the prize. And that prize is seeing Nico well and happy again. Helping him to handle his newfound status as the Blackstone heir. And making this palace a home, somehow.

But as her tired mind finally drifted into sleep it wasn't Nico's face she saw, but Lukas's. The jagged scar on his cheek tensed with barely leashed control.

The potent hunger in his dark eyes made her whole body yearn for things—scary things—she had no experience of. But far worse was the echo of longing which she'd thought she'd destroyed years ago, when she'd stood on her father's doorstep and willed him to look at her— and he never had.

CHAPTER FOUR

As THE NEXT few days and weeks unfolded, Bronte adapted to the staggering change in her and Nikky's circumstances with more ease than expected—because all her energies were focused on his treatment.

The morning after she had arrived at their new home she received the longed-for call from Dr Patel to confirm that Lukas was the partial match they needed for the experimental treatment. The following days spun past in a whirlwind of activity at the hospital, punctuated by long agonising waits, as Nico was prepped for surgery, given the life-altering graft of new bone marrow and then moved to an isolation chamber for his recovery.

Maureen and Lisa, the new team of bodyguards and the impressive support team Lukas had put in place handled all the niggling details of everyday life as Bronte devoted herself to being there for Nico.

She left the house early each morning in a chauffeur-driven car, was hustled through the phalanx of reporters and paparazzi who hadn't been put off by Lukas's press conference, and returned late each night—exhausted but ever more hopeful as each day passed.

Nico did his bit, responding wonderfully to the treatment. A few weeks after the operation he was already well enough to have a few carefully vetted visitors. Maureen, the staff from his old nursery school, Manny and the bouncer from the Firelite Club where she used to work. Even Lisa and some of the new staff at the house popped in to see him.

The only person who never appeared was Lukas.

At first, Bronte had been pathetically grateful he had kept his distance—the myriad confusing, conflicting and disturbing emotions he inspired not something she wanted to deal with. But as Nico recovered in leaps and bounds she began to feel less relieved at Lukas's continued absence from their lives.

Because Nico asked about his uncle constantly. The little boy had obviously latched on to Lukas, despite the tycoon's one perfunctory five-minute interaction with him.

As the weeks turned to months and Nico became well enough to return to his new home, Bronte's relief at Lukas's absence turned to guilt and concern.

In the two press conferences he'd given to control the media furore—in the early days before and then the weeks after Nico's operation—Lukas hadn't even mentioned his part in the boy's treatment and recovery.

Bronte had tried to contact him several times, to thank him for the bone marrow donation and update him on Nico's progress during his recovery, but Lisa, who had been assigned the job of being Bronte's point of contact with Lukas, hadn't been able to get him to respond in person to any of Bronte's news or enquiries.

She supposed she'd agreed to that too, that day in the waiting room, but she wasn't convinced Lukas's absence was the best thing for Nico any more as time passed. Eventually, Nico would wonder why Lukas never came to visit him. And she didn't want him to feel unwanted or inadequate, the way she had been made to feel by her own father's rejection.

Lukas Blackstone was Nico's uncle—and Nico's only connection to the man who had sired him—which meant, as far as Bronte was concerned, he was going to have to make more of an effort. Or Nico would suffer.

She was pondering the increasingly intransigent problem of Nico's absentee uncle one bright autumnal afternoon, nearly two months after the little boy had left hospital, as she watched Maureen show Nico how to make her famous sugar cookies, when the buzz of the kitchen phone snapped her out of her thoughts.

'Bronte, it's Dr Patel. I've just got Nico's latest lab results back and it's great news.'

Bronte's stomach lifted into her throat. 'Yes?'

'He's in complete remission.'

The words reverberated in her skull, bouncing around like teenagers at a rave. Bronte sat down heavily in the chair by the phone. 'That's wonderful—what does that mean?' she added as she sent a thumbs-up to Maureen, who was watching her encouragingly.

'It's basically the best news possible,' Dr Patel announced on the other end of the line. 'Obviously he'll need to continue having regular check-ups for a while, so his progress can be monitored. But we're not expecting any problems. Given the success of the treatment so far we have no reason to believe this isn't the cure we were hoping for.'

They talked for a few moments more, Bronte only managing to effectively process about half of the information. Her eyes stung as she replaced the phone in its stand.

Nico's dark head bent next to Maureen's grey hair as he concentrated on cutting dinosaur shapes out of the cookie dough. Autumn sunshine streamed through the windows, giving his chestnut curls a healthy glow.

Bronte blinked furiously to stop the happy tears from falling. Everything had been going so well, but this… This was freedom. It was a new start. A future.

'Can I eat the dough?' Nico pestered Maureen, gloriously oblivious to the enormity of the news they had just received, while the older woman placed the cookies in the oven.

'No dough, sweetheart—it has raw egg in it. Why don't you help me clean up the mess?' Maureen said.

Nico bobbed his head enthusiastically, then set about making more mess than he was actually clearing up—while Maureen spoke to Bronte in a hushed tone. 'Good news?'

'The best.' Bronte's eyes welled again, and Maureen walked over to wrap a warm arm round her shoulders. She handed Bronte a tissue.

'Why don't you take a moment, dear? I can get Nico fed and bathed and into bed tonight.'

'Are you sure?' Bronte said, blowing her nose.

'Of course I'm sure. You've been with him all day— you're entitled to a break too, you know?'

Brushing the specks of flour off her jeans, Bronte stood up.

'Okay, thanks,' she said, feeling way too tearful. She didn't want Nico to see her being over-emotional. She had been striving for as normal an environment as possible over the last two months since he'd returned home. Well, as normal as she could be when they were living in a twenty-eight-and-a-half-million-pound palace in Regent's Park.

'I should probably contact Lisa to let her know the news,' Bronte added.

So Lisa could relay it to the man who would not speak to them, she thought as she gave Nico a quick cuddle, which made him giggle.

Leaving the room, she headed up the kitchen stairs to the mansion's ground floor.

She entered the huge double-height reception room which she and Maureen had transformed into a cosy yet airy play area and family living space.

She loved this room. With two big comfy sofas, a child-sized desk and chair and Nico's favourite toys and games and a range of art supplies piled onto shelves built into the room's alcoves plus a fireplace with a childproof guard, it was the perfect space for her and Nico to hang out each afternoon when she collected him from the private nursery he attended around the corner.

She pulled out her mobile and keyed in Lisa's number but, as her thumb hovered over the call button, Bronte's heart thudded painfully and the conversation she would have with the personal assistant played through her mind. She would give Lisa her news, the woman would promise to pass it on to Lukas and try to get him to return her call in person—which they both knew he wouldn't do.

You're just as much of a coward as he is, Bronte O'Hara.

Wasn't she facilitating his non-involvement in Nico's life, by agreeing to relay all the essential information through Lisa? Lisa had told her a week ago Lukas was based in London at the moment, using the Blackstone Park Lane as his home base while he toured Blackstone's European properties. Lisa had, of course, attempted to persuade him to visit them in Regent's Park—but no such visit had been forthcoming. Bronte had no doubt at all that Lisa had tried, but as Lukas's employee it was hardly her job to persuade her billionaire boss to do something he didn't want to do.

Bronte's insides turned over as she switched off the phone and stuffed it back into her pocket.

This was ridiculous. She had incredible news. News that Lukas Blackstone was mostly responsible for. She had to stop letting him use Lisa as a buffer. And she had to stop using Lisa as a buffer herself.

It was time for her to man up and face her own demons. So what if she'd had that silly emotional blip—and all but melted into a puddle of unrequited need—the last time she'd been alone in a room with the man face to face. She'd been stressed beyond belief at the time and overwhelmed by the sudden twists and turns that his presence in her and Nico's lives represented.

But she was over that now. Nico was well again, and they were settled and happy in the house Lukas had purchased for them. He needed to hear how his nephew was doing from her—and he needed to man up too and be told in no uncertain terms that Nico needed him to be so much more than just a bottomless bank account.

If Lukas Blackstone still wanted to blank them both after that, then so be it. She couldn't force him to be present in Nico's life. But, for all their sakes, she had to at least try.

Texting Dave, their chauffeur, she headed out of the family room and grabbed her jacket.

Time's up, Lukas Blackstone. I'm not scared of you or my reaction to you any more.

Or not much, she thought, as she planted her bottom on the Mercedes' soft leather seat and the hot brick in her stomach became wedged in her throat.

CHAPTER FIVE

'I DON'T GIVE a damn how my dating life is going to play with the family demographic, Dex. Your job is to make sure it's not an issue.' Lukas balanced the phone between his collarbone and his chin and undid the cuffs of his shirt.

He'd flown in from Paris an hour ago in the company helicopter and he needed a shower. He was supposed to be attending a function tonight in the ballroom downstairs to launch the new branding for Blackstone's Deluxe Family Resorts. The build in the Maldives on the first resort was finally finished, but they had only a couple of months till the opening and there were still a ton of problems with the PR campaign. The top one of which was that his publicity guru Dex Garvey thought he could butt into Lukas's personal life to find a great angle to push their social media outreach.

'What about the pretty little thing you kissed at the Ball months ago?' Garvey jumped right back in, not deterred in the least by Lukas's sharp tone. 'She's your nephew's aunt, right? That Cinderella story has legs, Lukas. The press are still gagging for stories about the girl and the kid. And the speculation about what's going on between the two of you hasn't died down either. I heard the boy's out of hospital and home now in the place you bought for them. Why the heck don't you take her and the kid with you to the resort before it launches? We could get a photographer out there to document the whole thing. The press will lap it up and the social media buzz we could generate would be priceless.'

'I don't need priceless social media buzz. I need you to do your job and stop bugging me with this stuff.'

He hadn't seen Bronte O'Hara or his nephew since the day he'd brought her back to the UK from Manhattan. Had made a point of not having any contact with her or the boy. The fact that his thoughts often strayed to the memory of the child's hands wrapped around his waist during their one brief meeting, or that he still woke up most nights, his body hard and aching, with the memory of Bronte's taste lingering on his tongue was not significant. And certainly not something he planned to encourage.

The kid had gotten to him momentarily, because it had been a tough situation and the boy looked uncannily like his twin brother. The brother he'd never had the time or the inclination to grieve. Those dumb feelings of protectiveness towards the boy's aunt, the desire to make sure she was well cared for, had to be a result of that jolt too. And maybe transference. Somehow during their argument he'd mixed up his responsibilities for the welfare of Alexei's son with a responsibility he didn't even have for Bronte's welfare. His weird erotic obsession with the woman was even easier to explain. He hadn't gotten laid in months, and certainly not since he'd faced off with Bronte in the hospital waiting room. Maybe he'd find a willing woman at tonight's event and end the drought. Problem solved.

He shrugged out of his shirt.

'I'm just saying,' Garvey put on his wheedling voice,

the one that had helped win him accolades all over the globe for his media campaigns, and made him someone Blackstone's had spent a fortune head-hunting two years ago—something Lukas was starting to regret.

'I'm not gonna lie to you, Lukas. Your rep and the company's image took a hit when you decided not to get cosy with your new nephew. And his surrogate mommy.'

'I'm not the family man type, Garvey.' And he never would be. Families, how they operated, what they had to offer, didn't interest him. The bankrupt way his own family had operated had proved that to him years ago. 'Get over it and find another way to promote the new brand.'

'But you *are* the Blackstone brand.' Garvey whined some more. 'I still don't get why you wouldn't at least let me tell the media you're the anonymous donor that made the kid's treatment a success.'

'Because it's nobody's business.' And it would make him feel like a fraud. His involvement in Nico's treatment was just a trick of genetics. He sure as heck wasn't about to get business capital out of his arbitrary role in saving the boy's life. 'I'll see you in the ballroom in an hour—and I don't want to hear another word about this, or I'm going to reconsider the six-figure salary we're paying you.'

The heavy sigh down the line made Lukas bristle. But then Dex murmured, 'Yes, boss.'

Switching off the phone, Lukas finished undressing then stepped into the shower cubicle and turned the water jets to frigid. Just the mention of Bronte had had a predictable effect. Taking the erection in hand, he did what he'd been doing far too often of late. The perfunctory pleasure washed through him—but he knew it wouldn't be enough to satisfy the craving for long.

Whatever she'd done to him he needed to undo, to-night—or he was liable to lose his mind completely.

And if Dex brought up her name again, Blackstone's was finding a new PR guru.

'I need to see him, Lisa. I know you've done your best but he seems determined not to even acknowledge Nico's existence. Could you get me into his office?'

Lisa nodded. 'I understand, but he's not in his office.'

'He's not? Where is he?'

'In his suite on the top floor of the hotel, getting ready for tonight's launch for the new Blackstone Family Resort in the Maldives.'

'Oh.' Bronte's chest imploded like a burst balloon. 'I see.' She couldn't confront him in his private apartment— even the thought of it had the hot brick in her stomach sinking deeper into her abdomen. 'I guess I'll have to come back tomorrow.' And work herself up all over again. Somehow. 'Will he still be in London?'

'I think he's due to fly out to the Maldives tomorrow afternoon,' Lisa said, the sympathy in her eyes making Bronte feel like even more of a dope—for charging into the woman's office at six o'clock with no clear plan and no real clue. She should have made an appointment.

'Is everything okay with Nico?' Lisa asked.

'Yes, everything's really good. That's what I wanted to talk to Lukas about. Nico just got the all-clear from the hospital.'

'But that's wonderful news.' Lisa got up and walked round her desk.

Dressed in a red satin sheath dress, she looked im-maculate, her hair and make-up suggesting she had been about to leave for the press launch herself when Bronte had stormed into her office.

Bronte winced at the flour stains on her T-shirt and the mud on her jeans from where she'd been playing in the park with Nico that afternoon.

'I should go. I'm sorry to have bothered you,' Bronte said, her confidence and determination seeping away. 'Could you tell him I was here and give him the news?'

'Bronte—wait.' Lisa touched Bronte's arm as she turned to leave. 'I think you should tell him.'

'I know, but he's not here.' And the last of her confidence had already sunk into the toes of her muddy boots. However well she might have settled into the house in Regent's Park, however confident she felt in her role as Nico's guardian, she didn't belong in Lukas Blackstone's world and she never would. Nico would have to one day, and she'd do her best to prepare him for that, when the time came. But the time did not have to be now.

'Nonsense, he's right upstairs,' Lisa said, looking determined as she steered Bronte out of her office towards a bank of lifts. With night falling over Hyde Park, the suite of offices was virtually empty. Lisa led her up a small flight of stairs to a separate lift with a bronze plaque above it marked 'Penthouse only'. 'He's not due at the event for at least thirty minutes, which gives you plenty of time to talk to him alone and uninterrupted.'

Lisa whisked a small card out of the jewelled clutch purse which matched her sleek outfit and swiped it through a sensor on the lift panel. A bell dinged and the lift doors opened with an efficient swish.

'This is your chance. To talk to him about Nico.' She gave Bronte a gentle shove into the mirrored interior of the penthouse elevator. 'And stop him from avoiding you both. He's more interested in you two than he wants to let on,' Lisa added.

'What makes you think that?' Bronte asked, her thighs

starting to tremble. Was she really ready to meet Lukas Blackstone in the flesh again? To have another confrontation with him? Especially unaccompanied? In his penthouse? Could she trust all those unbidden thoughts and desires from their meeting months ago in the hospital waiting room not to burst out of hiding?

'Because he never misses an opportunity to ask after you both and he always listens intently to everything I tell him, not just about Nico but also about you,' Lisa said, the sympathy and understanding in her voice disturbing Bronte even more.

She didn't want Lukas to have an interest in her.

The surge of something hot and fluid made the earthquake in her knees hit nine point five on the Richter Scale and her heart kick her ribs in hard heavy thuds, calling her a liar.

'After working with him for five years,' Lisa continued, 'I can tell you he's a man who keeps his thoughts and feelings better guarded than Fort Knox. But I think he cares for you two. Or he would, if he gave himself a chance.'

'I'm really not sure this is a good idea,' Bronte said limply, wanting to step off the lift and run like hell, but unable to make her shaking legs move.

Leaning into the lift, Lisa used the card again and stabbed a button marked 'Private'.

'I get that,' Lisa said as she stepped back. 'But I'm ready to stake my job on being right.' A smile flickered across her face. 'And I'm sick to death of him using me as a go-between. Good luck.'

The doors swished closed, trapping Bronte in the lift alone.

Thirty seconds later, she stepped out into the palatial lobby area of a stunning penthouse apartment, completely convinced she was about to make the biggest mistake of her life.

Floor-to-ceiling glass panelling afforded a stunning view of Hyde Park as night drew in, floodlights illuminating Marble Arch in the distance through the trees. Muted lighting gave the flooring a mirrored sheen. A newsreader's voice droned as financial statistics scrolled over the flat-screen TV on the far wall.

'Hello? Lukas?' she called out in a tremulous whisper. She cleared her throat and tried again, glancing up the staircase leading to a mezzanine level.

'Bronte…?' Her head swung round so fast at the gruff enquiry from behind her she was lucky not to get whiplash.

Heat roared up from her core to incinerate every one of her pulse points at the sight before her.

Lukas Blackstone was naked, apart from a damp towel wrapped around his hips. He stood staring at her, his long hair-dusted legs apart, guarding a doorway that led into the dimly lit interior of a bedroom suite. Her gaze devoured the sleek musculature of his chest. Each bulge glistened with droplets of water, drawing her gaze down to the even more perilous territory of his hips. The man had a V so magnificent every drop of moisture in her mouth dried to dust. Magic fairy dust that made her tongue tickle with the urge to lick the water off those spectacular abs and delve down to…

She gulped audibly, becoming light-headed as every molecule of blood in her head plunged south.

'What are you doing here?' he said, his voice so husky it seemed to reverberate against her aching clitoris. 'Is there a problem with Nico?'

Nico. Yes, Nico. Nico is why I'm here. Isn't it?

The thought skittered across her mind but, as she tried

to grab hold of it and cling on, her gaze roamed up to his face and another blast of heat surged south.

'Nico's good,' she said. 'He's wonderful.' She had something specific to tell him about Nico but, whatever it was, it had been incinerated in the inferno now blazing through her body, leaving her mind clinging on to one thought, and one thought only.

I want to explore the ridged muscles of that eight pack with my tongue.

She forced her gaze to remain on his face, her breathing becoming rapid and uneven as she saw the same burning desire reflected back at her—in the rigid flex of the scar tissue tightening over his jaw, the bob of his Adam's apple, and the growing bulge lifting the towelling.

She stood frozen, crippled by her own yearning as he crossed the room. And cursed under his breath.

'You shouldn't have come,' he said, the words ripped from his throat.

Knowledge arched between them. Dark, driven and unstoppable. And she knew no force on earth would be able to stop her from giving into the need pounding hard enough to hurt in her sex.

'I know,' she said, her gaze fixed on his as his fingers curled around her upper arm and he drew her against naked flesh.

'I stayed away from you, dammit,' he growled, bending to press his face into her hair and skim his lips under her ear. 'Precisely so this wouldn't happen.'

'I'm sorry,' she said, because she could hear the edge of anger, although she wasn't sure what she was apologising for.

Her pulse battered her neck with the force and fury of a jackhammer.

He wanted her too. She hadn't imagined it.

Taking a deep breath in, he nuzzled the sensitive flesh beneath her chin, then finally found his way to her mouth.

She opened for him on a gasp of need, her legs giving way as his tongue explored and exploited, capturing her sobs. The hard length pressed against her belly, growing thicker and longer while the kiss became carnal and possessive.

Callused hands cradled her cheeks as he lifted his head, her panting breaths matched by the rasps of his. Those dark eyes searched her face, the intensity searing her skin and making the heat between her thighs go molten.

'Why did you come?' he asked.

She wanted to tell him she'd come for Nico. But in that moment the longing inside her was so huge it obliterated everything else. So she told him the truth. Or at least the part of the truth that couldn't hurt her.

'Because I want to make love to you.'

I want you to show me how. I want you to be my first.

As the thought entered her consciousness, she convinced herself that was all this was.

He choked out a harsh laugh, touched his forehead to hers, his hands roaming down to capture her backside and drag her more firmly against the thick bulge under his towel.

'I don't make love, Bronte. If that's what you want, you're looking in the wrong place.' The words were filled with a brittle conviction that made complete sense to her in that moment. This yearning for him wasn't emotional—it was physical. It was about finally giving in to the insane sexual chemistry which had been there from the first moment he'd touched her.

'It's just an expression,' she murmured, letting her hands flatten against the warm skin of his abdomen.

The muscles bunched and shuddered as she explored the firm flesh.

The surge of power was sweet and unprecedented, sweeping away the last of her fears and insecurities. Why couldn't she have this? Why did it have to mean anything?

Snagging her wrist, he headed towards the bedroom suite. He shut the door behind them and leaned back against it as she stood in the centre of the room.

He folded his arms over that magnificent chest. 'Prove it.'

'Prove what?' she said as she wrapped her arms around herself, the insecurities flooding back. Could he see how inexperienced she was, how unsure?

His head ducked, taking in her clothing. 'Show me this is what you want. Show me it's just sex,' he murmured, his voice so rough it felt like sandpaper scraping over every inch of exposed skin. 'Take off your clothes for me, Bronte.'

A violent tremble racked her body at the demand. She'd never undressed in front of any man before. But with the apprehension came the insistent well of desire. And she forced herself to unlock her arms, to stand proud.

He was challenging her, deliberately trying to frighten her off. Trying to take the power back that she'd seized moments before—trying to control her and the hunger between them. Her gaze fixed on the huge bulge, the towel now tented at an obscene angle.

His need was something he couldn't disguise. She forced herself to fix on that, and the clenching in her sex, the visceral desire to feel that powerful length inside her and not the fear demolishing her confidence.

She squeezed her trembling fingers into fists and shrugged off her jacket. Gripping the hem of her T-shirt, she dragged the cotton over her head and dropped it on the floor. Her skin tightened, the whisper of sensation becoming a roar as her breasts swelled and throbbed, the tips now painfully erect.

'Don't you dare stop,' he said, the demand edged with desperation.

So what if he'd dated supermodels? He was focused on her now. That intense gaze raked over sensitive flesh, the fight for control he was waging making her feel invincible.

Her muddy jeans and boots and the white sports bra probably wasn't the most seductive outfit, but his husky groan of encouragement spurred her on.

She fumbled with the buttons on her jeans and inched them down her hips. But as the denim snagged on her knees she realised too late she still had her boots on.

She fumbled and pushed at them. But she was stuck fast. Embarrassment scorched her insides. Who was she kidding? She didn't know what the heck she was doing, and now he would know that too…

But instead of laughing at her, or calling her out for being the fraud she was, he stalked towards her.

'To hell with this,' he snarled. 'I can't wait any longer.'

Pushing her back onto the bed, he yanked at her laces, then tugged her boots and jeans and panties off with feral efficiency. The towel dropped away as he climbed on top of her, his big body pressing her down into the mattress, the turgid erection brushed against her thigh. Droplets of water from his hair touched her breasts. The snap as her bra released echoed against the rasps of her breathing.

Her fingers dived into the damp silky locks of his hair as his tongue flicked over one turgid nipple. She arched into his mouth, her body begging for more. As if he could read her mind, he captured the peak with his lips, the strong suction sending heat spiralling into her already wet and willing sex.

She bucked off the bed, soaring as blunt fingers found her slick folds. She sobbed. The feel of his fingers stretching her, driving her, his thumb circling, teasing, torturing.

Her nails scored down his back. It was too much. And yet not nearly enough.

'Please...' she moaned, scared to let go yet desperate to feel him there. Everywhere.

Sensation swelled and peaked—eddying out in undulating waves—as he finally found the heart of her with his thumb. She floated for one precious moment in a sparkling dream. Then crashed to earth, the glorious pleasure breaking over her.

He swore, and she could hear her own desperation of moments before in the fierce tone. Rolling her over, he drew her up on her knees. Like a rag doll, her will no longer her own, she allowed herself to be positioned, too drunk on afterglow to care as his muscular forearm banded round her waist and the huge head of his penis nudged her sex from behind.

She tensed against the thick invasion as he pressed into her—slowly, surely, relentlessly, butting against the tiny barrier, he surged past it.

She cried out, the brutal pleasure turning to stretching pain. He was too big—she could feel every inch of him, lodged so deep inside her, the staggered breaths tearing at her chest.

His arm tightened around her midriff, his breathing harsh against her neck as he stilled. 'Bronte, what the—?' His grunt of shock was both raw and accusatory. 'Are you a virgin?'

She bit down on the urge to lie and deny it. It was

pointless being ashamed of her inexperience now. 'Not any more.'

He swore, and she got the opinion he didn't much appreciate her joke.

'Why didn't you tell me?' he demanded, still lodged inside her.

Her sex clenched and released, trying to bring back the glorious oblivion that had felt so good only moments before, but now made her feel overwhelmed, impaled.

'Because it was none of your business,' she said, wanting to sound tough, but the quiver in her voice was a dead giveaway.

'Am I hurting you?' he asked, moving his hand up to brush the hair away from her face.

She turned into his palm, not wanting him to see how overwhelmed she felt. 'No,' she said, wanting to mean it.

'Don't lie,' he murmured.

His hand caressed her cheek, then slid down to cradle her breast. He kissed the back of her neck while he toyed with the nipple. The light, teasing pressure sent ribbons of sensation shuddering down to her tender core.

'Maybe a little,' she admitted, the brusque show of tenderness even more excruciating than the interrogation.

His hand left her breast and slid down to her sex. She groaned, the ribbons of sensation sparking through her body as he found the tight bundle of nerves at the apex of her thighs.

She shuddered, her sex clasping hard now, massaging his penis.

'Better?' he asked, the strain in his voice matching her own.

'Yes,' she moaned. Her hips moved forward now, releasing the immense pressure, but then rocked back in a dangerous dance, her body greedy for its own destruction.

He used his thumb to stroke her into a frenzy, his own breathing rapid and uneven, but he didn't, didn't thrust. He let her control the dance. The pain receded but the discomfort remained—he still felt so large.

But gradually the pleasure built, the ribbons becoming whips, stinging her skin, scouring her inside, forcing her towards a new ecstasy, so much more agonising but so much more intense and glorious than what had gone before.

Finally, he began to move too, driving forward as she drove back, thrusting deeper, making her take all of him. Her mind drifted, dazed and yearning—the excruciating pleasure drawing tight—his thumb still concentrated on those traitorous nerve-endings.

Sweat slicked her skin, the sounds basic, elemental, animalistic as they both strived to reach that impossible peak. His penis nudged a spot deep inside and she jerked, staggered by the renewed sensation, the new surge of pleasure.

'There,' he grunted. 'That's it.'

And then he stroked the spot over and over again, pushing her into the maelstrom with those focused, relentless caresses.

She charged over that final edge, crying out as the pleasure cascaded through her like a meteor shower. Shattering her.

Hot seed exploded inside her as her muscles clamped tight, milking him. She collapsed forward and he collapsed on top of her, crushing her into the mattress, her body shuddering with the aftershocks of her climax. She felt the drawing pain as he shifted, the firm weight finally pulling out of her.

Dazed and disorientated by the enormity of what had

happened to her body, she found herself being lifted in strong arms.

He carried her into a tiled bathroom, the glint of graphite on the surfaces in the bright light blinding her before the lights dimmed.

Hot jets massaged her body, the scent of juniper and pine drifting around her as slick suds and firm hands soaped overused muscles and tender flesh. She bucked against his hold as he probed gently between her legs, touching, testing.

He swaddled her in a bath sheet, but even the soft towelling felt like too much sensation on her over-sensitised flesh. Carrying her back into the bedroom, he laid her on the bed.

'Wait here. I'm gonna take a shower and then we need to talk,' he murmured.

Talk? What was there to talk about?

The thought paralysed her for a moment. She watched him walk back into the bathroom, heat stinging her cheeks as she noticed the livid red marks on his back.

Did I do that?

Light gilded the tanned musculature and the tight orbs of his buttocks as he switched the light back up to glaring in the bathroom and closed the door. Arousal surged back into her too-tender flesh, making her flinch.

Down, girl—you're in no condition to even consider doing that again any time soon.

She wrapped herself in the towel, heard the water gushing from the power shower. She should get up, get dressed and leave, before he returned from the bathroom—she was too dazed right now to have a coherent conversation.

But her limbs felt heavy and uncoordinated and her mind numb, as the events of the last half hour spun through her brain—the pleasure and the pain, but most of all the brutal intimacy.

Her eyelids sunk to half-mast and her brain turned to mush as she tried to block out the kaleidoscope of images swirling in her head, both magnificent and terrifying.

She'd never realised sex would be so overwhelming, so overpowering, so all-consuming. She hadn't thought of Nico once, not since Lukas had appeared in his bedroom doorway with that excuse for a towel hooked round his waist.

All she'd been able to think about was feeding the hunger inside her. But that wasn't all she'd felt—there had been more to it than just the physical, and that was what terrified her most of all.

She was still wrestling with how to deal with that brutal feeling of vulnerability when Lukas reappeared from another door—fully clothed. He glanced her way while fixing cufflinks into a white shirt. Perfectly tailored tuxedo trousers emphasised the power in his long legs, while the bedroom's dim lighting shone on the thick waves of damp hair and the polished sheen of his loafers.

Bronte pushed herself into a sitting position, struggling to keep the towel covering all the essential bits. The heat stinging her cheeks spread like wildfire to burn her scalp.

One dark eyebrow lifted and a rueful smile tugged at his sensual lips. 'Still blushing, Bronte?'

She shook her head, not able to speak. He looked so magnificent, and so far out of her league. Had she really made love with this man? Lost her virginity to him? And what had happened to the power she'd revelled in while she was in his arms, because right this second she'd never felt more small or insignificant. Or powerless.

He sat beside her on the edge of the bed and stroked

a fingertip over her cheek, before hooking a lock of her hair behind her ear. The light, oddly possessive caress only triggered the terror crushing her chest again and the flush blazed back to life.

He let his hand drop, and she felt a strange sense of loss.

'I need to go to this dumb event. I'm late already. Does anyone know you're here?'

'Only Lisa,' she said.

That sceptical eyebrow rose again. 'Is she the one who gave you the access code to my private elevator?'

He didn't sound annoyed, only curious, but her insides twisted with guilt.

'I made her do it.' She couldn't bear it if Lisa lost her job over this. 'I wanted to talk to you about Nico,' she said, even though they both knew that was hardly the whole truth.

'What about Nico?'

'We got the all-clear from the hospital this afternoon. I thought you should know, seeing as you're such a large part of his recovery.'

The startled pleasure in his expression did nothing to ease the sharp feeling of fear and inadequacy. She didn't want to like him. Hadn't wanted this to mean more than sex…but somehow it did.

'Hardly,' he said. 'But thanks for letting me know. Although I'm not sure that required a personal visit.'

If he was teasing her it was hard to tell. As Lisa had said, he was a man capable of keeping his emotions guarded better than Fort Knox. But she thought she caught a flicker of amusement in his eyes. It gave her the courage to say what she should have said to him when she'd arrived.

'That's not the only reason I wanted to tell you in person. Nico asks about you constantly.'

'Seriously?' He sounded sceptical. 'He's only met me once.'

'I know, but he's got a little fixated on you.' She ducked her head, concentrating on the wad of towelling gripped in her fingers. Nico wasn't the only one who'd got fixated on Lukas Blackstone.

She forced her gaze back to his. 'You're his only male relative. And he knows the part you played in making him well again. I can't keep telling him you're too busy every time he asks to see you. Eventually he'll figure out you don't want to visit him. And then he'll start to wonder why. And I don't want him to think less of himself if he does.'

He watched her for the longest time, the knowledge in his eyes disconcerting. The flutter of panic that she might have said too much was even more so. Did he somehow know that her own father had deserted her and her sister?

But, as much as she wanted to, she refused to relinquish eye contact under that searching gaze.

Don't be ridiculous! How can he know? And, anyway, this is not about you—it's about Nico.

'I'm not cut out to be anyone's father,' he said at last.

He'd said something similar once before, and she'd accepted it without question then; this time she couldn't allow herself to be deterred so easily. For Nico's sake.

'No one's asking you to be his father, Lukas. But would it really be so hard to at least visit him occasionally? When you're in London? It would mean so much to him. And it would let him know he's wanted.'

It was Lukas's turn to look away—but not before she'd seen the uneasy expression. And forced herself to acknowledge a reality that had become blurred by their lovemaking.

Not lovemaking. Sex.

This was hard for Lukas. For whatever reason, he clearly didn't want to make a personal connection with the boy whose life he'd saved. His own brother's son. She needed to remember that, before she allowed the traitorous emotions that had crippled her once before when her father had rejected her to get out of hand again.

He sighed and scrubbed his hands down his face but, as he did so, it drew her attention to the scar that marred his cheek.

And the yearning she'd tried so hard to ignore, to pretend didn't exist, made her heart lurch into her throat.

Maybe he was invulnerable now, but he hadn't always been.

He checked his watch. 'Okay,' he said, his reluctance palpable. 'I'll visit the boy tomorrow morning, if you promise not to make too big a deal of it.'

'I won't,' she said, knowing full well that Nico would make a big enough deal of it for both of them. 'And thank you,' she added, knowing she'd won a major concession. Maybe Fort Knox wasn't as well fortified as it appeared.

But before she could process that disturbing thought he added, 'Talking of not wanting to be a father, I didn't use a condom earlier. Is that going to be a problem?'

The direct question—and the abrupt change of subject—left her reeling. The blush became radioactive. 'No,' she blurted out.

His gaze narrowed, as if he could see right through the show of bravado. 'Are you sure?' he asked. 'You're not exactly the most experienced woman I've ever slept with.'

'Yes, of course I'm sure,' she said, feeling defensive—

and hopelessly gauche and unsophisticated. 'Just because I'm a virgin, it doesn't make me an imbecile,' she added, protesting a little too much.

'*Were* a virgin,' he corrected, that tiny smile curving his lips again. 'So you're using contraceptive pills?' he reiterated.

'I said it won't be a problem,' she replied, not entirely truthfully. But she felt hideously exposed, her feelings raw and tender when they had no right to be. Especially in the face of his pragmatism.

She forced her pride to the fore, to cover the erratic beat of her heart.

She'd rather die than admit she wasn't on the Pill, that she hadn't even considered contraception. But she was so close to the end of her cycle, an accidental pregnancy had to be highly unlikely. And if any problems did arise, she told herself staunchly, she'd handle them. Alone. She might be inexperienced, but she wasn't naïve. She wasn't about to risk having another child. And especially not with a man like Lukas.

I don't make love.

She gripped the towel tighter around her, the chill in the room prickling over her skin. If there was one thing she'd learned from her father—and Darcy's brief but catastrophic affair with Lukas's brother—you couldn't make a man love you. And you certainly couldn't change him. Nor should you try to. It was far too much work, and it was bound to fail. Leaving you deluded, like Darcy, or destroyed, like their mother.

Maybe she'd lost sight of that in the heat of the moment. But she wasn't going to forget it again. She didn't need or want any man's love. She had Nico. And she had herself. And that was more than enough.

He watched her, as if he were trying to assess whether

to quiz her further. She knew she'd never been a very accomplished liar, so she drew her knees up to her chest, keeping the towel wrapped firmly around her. Not that it made her feel any less naked under that searing gaze.

'Shouldn't you be going to your event?' she prompted, suddenly desperate to escape from him, and all the feelings still churning inside her that had no right to be there. 'You're late already.'

'I want you here when I get back,' he said. Or rather demanded.

She bristled, not just at the dictatorial tone but the underlying suggestion—that somehow because she'd slept with him she was now his to command.

But she held on to the curt reply. She didn't have the energy to have a stand-off with him. Not only that, but she was naked while he was fully clothed, and the heat had begun to pulse in her sex again, as soon as he'd walked back into the room in that tux. She couldn't be sure she wouldn't dissolve into another puddle of lust if he pushed. And she didn't want to make love—correction, have sex with him again—until she'd got over the emotional fallout from their first encounter.

Of course, it hadn't meant anything to him—he'd had a ton of girlfriends. And he'd already told her he had a lot of experience separating sex from emotion. But he was her first. And it had been…well, pretty mind-blowing—in a purely physical sense. However pragmatic and practical and not naïve she was, losing your virginity to a man like Lukas Blackstone was bound to take a little while to process. And get in perspective.

Her skin flushed pink again. He stood up to leave, his big body towering over her.

Okay, make that a lot of time to process and get in perspective.

'I'll be back in half an hour at the most,' he said, as if she were a puppy who was expected to be obedient.

'I won't be here. I can't stay,' she said.

He frowned, his displeasure clear. 'Why not?'

'I have to get back to Nico. I always kiss him good-night.' It wasn't a lie, she told herself. She needed to see Nico tonight, now more than ever. The little boy would keep her grounded, stop her making too much of what had happened. Stop her wanting it to happen again, which would be catastrophic. She could see that already.

His frown deepened—he didn't like her excuse—but after what felt like several millennia he gave a brief nod. 'Okay, I'll see you tomorrow morning then.'

She felt the muscles in her abdomen loosen with relief.

'I'll come to the house. But I want to see you in private before I see the boy.'

'Why?' she asked.

His gaze raked down to where she held the towel too tightly against her chest. Her nipples throbbed and peaked in a predictable response.

'I think you can guess why, Bronte. You're not innocent any more.'

She wanted to be disgusted by his implication—that now they'd slept together once, she'd be happy to sleep with him again simply because he expected her to. But the only one she was disgusted with was herself. And her instinctive response to him.

She bristled, and clutched the towel tighter. 'All right,' she said, while planning to make sure she did not let Nico leave her side every moment Lukas was in the house.

Forget taking time to process the sex and get it into perspective. No time would be long enough to mitigate the erotic power he wielded over her.

Lukas was just too… Well, too everything. He was coming to the house to see Nico, not her—and once he left he was going to the Maldives. It would be weeks before he returned, by which time he would have forgotten about her and this…this *thing* between them. And, hopefully, with time and distance she would have too. And the erotic power he wielded would no longer be an issue. And all these raw, runaway emotions, the inexplicable yearning, would be gone too. Because they would both have moved on.

'Take the elevator down when you're ready,' he said, still ordering her about. 'I'll tell Lisa to arrange a car and have a couple of security guards standing by to usher you out the back entrance to avoid the press.'

'Okay,' she said, grateful that he'd considered the fallout if the press got hold of what had just happened. And adding it to the long list of reasons why having an affair with Lukas Blackstone would be a very bad idea.

But as he leant down to kiss her forehead his thumb lingered on the pulse in her collarbone. Her breath got trapped in her lungs, the hammering pulse in her neck matching the beating pulse in her clitoris as he stroked the soft skin with deliberate purpose.

'Later,' he murmured, the hunger in his eyes unmistakable, the sensual smile a come-on that told her he was well aware of the effect he had on her.

As he left the room longing seared her insides, and she knew Lukas's arrogant assumptions weren't going to be the only problem when it came to putting an end to this liaison.

Because by far the biggest problem was her own body's traitorous flash-fire response to him. And those volatile emotions that couldn't seem to accept this *thing* for what it was—which was nothing of any importance.

* * *

Lukas strode through the apartment lobby. He shouldn't have touched her, shouldn't have given in to the promise of those wide pouting lips, those sparkling emerald eyes, that artlessly responsive body—and that open and forthright spirit that had captivated him right from the start. If he'd known she was a virgin he wouldn't have gone near her.

But now he had there was no going back.

Because he couldn't un-touch her, or un-know her, or un-taste her—and the memory of the clasp of her sex, the sweetness of her nipples tightening beneath his tongue, the shuddering pants as he thrust inside her— even that sassy little reply when he'd asked her if she was a virgin...

Not any more.

...was already driving him nuts to have her again.

It was just sex, even if it was like no sex he'd ever had before. Nothing more than insane hormones and great chemistry. It would burn itself out eventually but, until it did, he wasn't risking going madder than he was already.

Bypassing the penthouse elevator as he always did, he shoved open the door to the emergency stairs. Jogging down twenty flights to the eleventh floor ballroom would go some way towards calming the heavy feeling in his guts.

Unfortunately, it couldn't make him forget the sight of her on his bed, wrapped in nothing but a towel, her huge eyes confused and wary, her pale, ethereal skin flushed with pleasure.

Her relationship with and devotion to the boy was a complication, of course, not to mention her virginity. Luckily, he had become an expert at keeping his feelings and his emotional needs—if he even had them any more, which was doubtful—strictly compartmentalised ever since he was a boy himself.

He never let people get too close because that just gave them the power to hurt and disappoint him. Opening the emergency exit, he stepped into the lobby. As he crossed the thick carpeting towards the ballroom entrance, he was soon spotted. Reporters and bloggers rushed towards him firing questions.

'Hey, Lukas, what's happening with your long-lost nephew? Any chance he'll be visiting the new resort with you?'

'Why the move into the family market when you don't have a family yourself, Lukas? Is there something you're not telling us?'

He stopped, and the young female vlogger who had asked the question stuck her phone in his face.

'You'll hear the reason why when you watch the presentation,' he said smoothly, although he was grateful when his well-trained security detail surrounded him because his blood pressure—and his irritation—was rising.

But as he continued into the ballroom, flanked by bodyguards, the flash and flare of camera phones and VT lights exploding in his face, the press of bodies, didn't bother him as much as they usually did because his mind was focused on Bronte again—the sobs of her arousal, that smart seductive mouth, that ripe responsive body, the firm set of her chin when he'd demanded she stay and she'd defied him.

A wry smile broke over his face at the thought of seeing her again tomorrow morning.

Keeping their affair secret from the press, getting Bronte to cooperate despite her obvious reluctance, and figuring out how to curb his involvement with the boy was going to be a tough juggling act. But having Bronte

O'Hara as his mistress for the next little while would be worth the effort.

No obstacle was going to be big enough to stop him from getting what he wanted. Because he now knew exactly how hot they were together. All he had to do was remind her of that—which wouldn't be a hardship. And make sure she understood that sex was all he could offer her. But really that shouldn't be a problem. For all her inexperience, Bronte was a realist, not a romantic.

He spotted his executive assistant in the melee as he approached the stage. His smile widened at Lisa's sheepish expression. If Bronte agreed to the proposition he was going to make to her tomorrow, the details of which he was already milling over in his mind, he might well have to give the woman a bonus.

CHAPTER SIX

By EIGHT-TEN THE next morning, Lukas wasn't feeling quite so magnanimous.

He'd woken early and after consulting with one of his estate managers he'd taken an unmarked SUV to the back entrance of the house in Regent's Park. He'd texted Bronte before he left to inform her he would be arriving in ten minutes and wanted an hour alone with her before he saw Nico. He had hoped to catch her in bed, the wintry dawn only an hour off daybreak.

Entering from the mews, he'd walked through the house's gardens to the kitchen door, eager to see Bronte, and take care of the ache that had kept him awake most of the night.

He had an email on his phone with links to a series of mews cottages in Chelsea for Bronte to choose from. Obviously he couldn't come here to see her—it would only confuse the boy and, anyway, for what he planned they would need complete privacy. But he was paying her friend Maureen a generous salary for her childcare expertise and the boy was four now and well again. It would do both Bronte and the child good to spend some time apart.

He knew this might be a sticking point for her because she was so devoted to the boy. But he was prepared to make concessions—limiting their liaison to one or two nights a week. They could do a lot in that time, given the right incentive.

The unbidden smile curled his lips again as he tapped on the back door. Instead of Bronte's slender frame, though, a middle-aged woman with warm grey eyes pulled it open. She looked vaguely familiar.

'Mr Blackstone, I'm so pleased to meet you at last,' she said. 'I'm Maureen Fitzgerald,' she added, reaching for his coat. 'Let me take your jacket. It's miserable weather out there this morning.' She carried on chatting about the rain—which he hadn't even noticed—as she placed his coat on a hook next to a tiny red raincoat and the jacket he had watched Bronte shrug out of yesterday. Equally tiny boots with a pink pig-like creature on them stood next to the battered leather boots he remembered yanking off Bronte the evening before.

The evidence of the child's existence and his attachment to Bronte gave Lukas an unpleasant jolt.

'Where's Bronte?' he asked—maybe she was still in bed, waiting for him. Was that why she hadn't greeted him?

'She's in the front parlour with Nico,' the woman said cheerfully, dashing his hopes as she guided him through the kitchen towards a staircase.

'The boy's awake already?' he said.

And why was the child with Bronte? Hadn't he specifically told her he wanted some time alone with her first?

'We've been up for several hours—it's past eight o'clock,' the woman said, leading him through the quiet house, the smell of fresh baking and lemon polish giving him a strange pang in his chest. 'Boys of four don't generally sleep past daybreak,' she added with a friendly smile that didn't quite hide the note of condescension. 'Even if they hardly slept a wink last night,' she added, still smiling at what had to be a private joke because he wasn't finding any of this remotely funny. 'Poor Bronte had to get up twice in the night to get him back into bed.'

'Why? Is the boy ill?' he asked, concern for the child's welfare taking him unawares. While he had no emotional attachment to his nephew, he didn't want the child to look as distressed and fragile as he had when Lukas had first met him.

'Oh, no,' Maureen chuckled. 'He's just over-excited.'

'What about?' he said as she opened a door and he heard the hum of voices—one high and childlike, the other smoky and feminine and very familiar.

'About your visit, of course,' the woman said as she ushered him into the room.

He located Bronte immediately. She sat cross-legged on a hearthrug, busy putting together a puzzle of what looked like a red sports car with a face. Her flaming hair and those tantalising freckles were gilded by the fire in the room's marble hearth as she turned her head towards him.

Everything seemed to slow inside him and then smack into a brick wall. The punch of lust hit like a lightning strike. Colour suffused her cheeks, making the freckles flicker like the flames in the grate—and he had to stop himself from marching across the room and flinging her over his shoulder, to take her back to the bed she should still have been in.

Three thoughts hit him at once.

Why the heck did the spark of defiance in her eyes turn him on even more? How was he going to curb this hunger? Because he already knew no way in hell was two nights a week going to be enough. And why did it feel as if it wasn't just the prospect of having sex with her again that was causing that deep throbbing ache in his gut?

But before he could even attempt to answer any of those questions, or demand to know why she hadn't met him alone as he'd requested, a dark head popped up from behind her.

'You came! You came! He came, Bronte. You said he would.'

High with excitement, the boy's shouts were followed by the pounding of his feet as he leapt up and ran towards Lukas at full pelt, scattering the puzzle pieces and every one of Lukas's thoughts, before thudding into him.

Lukas grunted, the child's head just narrowly missing butting him right in the crotch.

The sturdy body felt warm and alive against his legs but as Lukas bent, trying to grab hold of the wriggling figure before he did any serious damage, the boy's head lifted and he got his first good look at the child's face.

The shock made him stiffen.

Gone was the pallor and fragility of three months ago. Thank God. But now the resemblance to Alexei—probably to himself too—was that much more startling and unnerving. A thousand memories bombarded him.

Of Alexei hooting with laughter as they raced each other, sliding down the bannisters of their father's town house in Manhattan. Alexei's screams echoing off the sidewalk as hard hands gripped Lukas's arm and wrenched it so hard he passed out. Alexei crying, his fingers touching the bandages on Lukas's face, as his brother snuggled next to him on his hospital bed.

Darker, more dangerous memories lurked at the edge of his consciousness—searing pain, the acrid smell of vomit and blood and urine, and the impenetrable terrifying darkness closing in on him.

He drew away from the boy, the fight to keep the memories back almost as huge as the gaping hole in his heart where his brother had once been.

'Lukas, is everything okay?' Bronte's voice, gentle and thick with concern, beckoned him out of the darkness.

She came forward, the worry on her face reflecting his own shattered thoughts. Her hand rose, reaching out. And for one terrifying moment all he wanted was to grab hold of her fingers and have her pull him back towards the light.

But instead she gripped the boy's shoulder and tugged him back, away from Lukas. He felt the loss of warmth, of connection, like a blow.

'Lukas?' she said again as she held the boy's shoulders. 'Is something the matter?'

They were both looking at him expectantly, the boy's eyes widening with a vivid combination of childish curiosity and fascination. He locked the yearning back inside. Humiliated.

'Of course not,' he snapped, because for the first time in a very long time he didn't feel okay—he felt broken again.

The boy flinched and jerked further away from him into Bronte's arms—all the childish excitement of moments before extinguished in a heartbeat.

Lukas winced, hearing the cruel echo of his father's voice in his own. And regret crushed his chest. He'd messed up. He let his hand drop and glanced at Bronte, unsure of what to do next.

He had no experience with children whatsoever. And he'd obviously frightened the boy. He wanted to make it right.

'I'm sorry,' he said, keeping his voice soft, and for the first time in a long time letting his uncertainty show. 'What should I do?'

* * *

'Nico, it's okay. Lukas didn't mean to scare you.' Bronte ran her hand over Nico's hair and kept her voice light, even though her heart was pounding so hard she could hardly breathe.

Lukas had looked stricken when Nico had embraced him. She'd realised in that moment, his reluctance to come here, to visit Nico, wasn't about selfishness, or convenience, or a lack of emotion on his part. It might well be the opposite.

She shook off the dangerous thought.

Don't think about that now.

She knew Lukas's barked remark had startled Nico, but she doubted there was any permanent damage. Nico was just tired and way too overexcited, never a great combination for an active four-year-old. But now she had to convince Lukas he hadn't done something monstrous by being a little short with his nephew.

Kneeling down, Bronte gave Nico an easy hug and tapped her finger on his nose, pushing a lightness she didn't feel into her tone. 'You know what, Nikky,' she continued. 'Lukas said he was sorry to you, so I think maybe you should say sorry to him.'

'Why?' Nico said with the bluntness of all four-year-olds.

'That's really not necessary,' Lukas said at the same time, his frown making Bronte's heart pound even harder.

She knew she needed to be careful not to read too much into his eagerness to make amends. But there was something so endearing about seeing Lukas stick up for the little boy who was a childlike image of himself—especially as she suspected he very rarely, if ever, had to second-guess himself, or apologise to anyone.

Bronte cleared her throat, determined to unblock the

emotion lodged there. 'You want Lukas to play with you, don't you?' Bronte said, addressing Nico.

Nico considered the question and she could feel the tension in Lukas as he waited for the boy's answer. Nico nodded.

She swallowed to release the blockage. 'Then you need to say hello properly, and ask him nicely,' she said. 'Running up and shouting at him probably scared him a little too.'

Nico stared at Lukas. 'I'm sorry I scared you. I didn't mean to.'

Lukas's lips twitched; he was clearly seeing the absurdity of the situation. 'That's really okay. I'm good now,' he said gravely, and she had to stem the insane urge to hug this taciturn man for treating Nico's apology with the gravity it deserved. However absurd.

'Do you want to come play with my Lego?' Nico said, getting more animated, his caution disappearing as quickly as it had come.

'Sure.'

Before Lukas had a chance to say more, Nico had gripped his hand and was tugging him across the room towards the house he was currently making for Dora the Explorer.

Bronte's heartbeat stuttered and stumbled as she watched Lukas fold his long frame into the child-sized chair next to Nico's. The furniture creaked under his weight as he spread his legs out under the table in a futile bid to get comfortable. He bent his head next to his nephew's and the two of them began sorting through the colourful plastic bricks together, Nico chatting away about Dora and Lukas nodding and clearly struggling to keep up with the flow of information. She swallowed furiously, then noticed the way Lukas's black cashmere sweater tightened around his broad shoulders as he leant forward to grab a particular brick. The familiar heat surged.

Stop it.

She tore her eyes away from him.

She'd wanted Lukas to bond with Nico, but she did not need to bond with him too. The hot, focused look he'd given her before Nico had barrelled into him had been enough to prove to her she needed to keep her distance today.

'Can you come see me tomorrow?' Nico stretched his arms above his head and opened his mouth in a yawn so big it was a wonder he didn't dislocate his jaw.

'I can't,' Lukas said, but Bronte couldn't help noticing his look of dismay when Nico's face fell comically. 'I have business in the Maldives for a few weeks.'

'Where's the Maldives?' the little boy asked.

'It's in the Indian Ocean.'

'Can I come with you?'

'Um…' Lukas stalled again, clearly not knowing what to say, and Bronte felt her heart stutter again, as it had been doing all morning.

Lukas had surprised her. He'd been patient and approachable and attentive in the past two hours with the little boy, fielding endless questions, listening to Nico's rambling conversation on everything from his nursery school teacher to his favourite TV shows, while diligently building a veritable Lego conurbation for Dora the Explorer and all her friends. But as she watched Lukas struggle to answer this latest question, clearly weighing up what to say, Bronte suspected the person Lukas had surprised most was himself.

Despite his reluctance to come here, and what she now suspected was his initial moment of panic when Nico had greeted him so enthusiastically, Lukas had bonded this morning with his brother's son—and comprehensively lost the battle he had been waging up to now not to engage with Nico. Making her all the more curious about why Lukas had been so determined not to make that connection.

'Stop badgering your uncle, munchkin,' she said, taking pity on Lukas. She leant over Nico from the other side of the bed and lifted the covers to tuck them securely around him.

'Aw but…' Nico began.

'Not another word.' She tapped his nose with her fingertip. 'You need to go to sleep.'

'But I'm not even tired,' the boy said around another huge yawn. 'And I don't want Uncle Lukas to go away. Because then I'll never see him again.'

The pang hit Bronte squarely in the chest—the yearning in Nico's voice echoing thoughts and feelings of her own that she knew she couldn't afford to acknowledge.

'I'll come back to visit when I return,' Lukas offered and Bronte felt her heart thud in her throat, her emotions in turmoil again. She wanted to encourage Lukas's involvement with Nico, especially as she could already see how beneficial this connection could be, not just for Nico but for Lukas too. But by sleeping with him last night, she had complicated the situation immeasurably.

Her awareness of him all morning had only added to her turmoil. Watching him interact with Nico with such surprising tenderness and sensitivity had only made the desire rippling over her skin every time she felt his gaze on her—watching and assessing—that much more acute. How was she supposed to resist this yearning, to keep the barriers in place she'd been struggling to erect all morning, if she began to like him, as well as desire him?

'Do you promise?' the little boy said, the excited tone making the pang in Bronte's chest sharpen.

'You have my word,' Lukas said, the solemn tone making it clear his word was something he didn't give lightly, and would never break.

Nico's eyes widened with a look that could only be described as awestruck.

'Now do what your aunt tells you, and go to sleep,' Lukas added. He levered himself off the bed, but then reached out to ruffle the boy's hair in an impromptu gesture which seemed to surprise him as much as Nico.

The light, fleeting touch was like a magic wand.

'Yes, Uncle Lukas,' Nico mumbled, his eyelids drooping before he rolled over in the bed and dropped into sleep, obeying the command without question.

Lukas's dark gaze connected with hers from across the bed as she stood too. The heat between them—that had been simmering beneath the surface all through the morning—flared to life. And the memory of another promise—to talk to Lukas privately before he met Nico today—screamed across the distance between them.

Flustered and far too aware of all the reasons why she did not want to risk having that conversation now, when her emotions were even more volatile than they had been last night, Bronte shot towards the door.

'I'll see you out,' she said. 'Maureen said your driver is waiting to take you to the airport.'

He had a flight to catch. They didn't have time to talk about anything. She was safe for today. Nico and his boundless energy and excitement at meeting Lukas properly for the first time had saved her, as she knew it would. She stifled the prickle of guilt. This visit was always supposed to be about Nico's relationship with Lukas, not hers. Not that she even had a relationship with him. Not one she intended to pursue anyway.

But as she darted ahead of Lukas, strong fingers snagged her wrist—and drew her to a sudden halt.

'Not so fast. Aren't you forgetting something?' The tone was curt.

'I don't think so,' she said, tugging on her wrist.

Ignoring her struggle, he dragged her into a room across the hall.

Shutting the door behind them, he spun her round. Her back butted against the door. Placing his hands above her head, he caged her in and a familiar surge of heat soared up her torso to ignite her cheeks and send her senses into turmoil—right alongside her emotions.

'Lukas! You don't have time for this,' she said, trying for exasperated but getting breathless instead.

His brows slammed down in a furious frown. 'You little... You planned this deliberately, didn't you?' he growled, his juniper and pine scent surrounding her now—rich and evocative and far too enticing.

'I don't know what you mean,' she said, attempting to duck out from under his arm, frantic to escape before the heavy weight in her sex, the sharp tug of arousal overrode her flight instinct again.

'The hell you don't...' he said, planting large palms on her hips and holding her firmly in place. 'You knew I wanted to talk to you this morning about us. You used the boy as a shield. Admit it.'

She flattened her hands against his chest. The muscles rippled with tension beneath the soft cashmere but, instead of pushing him away as she should, her body shuddered with yearning.

'There is no us.' She forced herself to meet his gaze.

'The only connection we have is through Nico,' she added, wanting to mean it, wanting to believe it. 'He's the only thing that matters now. And you were so brilliant with him today.'

His brows lifted and she pounced on the opportunity to distract him, and herself. And resist the yearning that was threatening to consume her again.

'I don't want to do anything to threaten your relationship with him.' At least that wasn't a lie.

Pursuing a relationship with Lukas, any kind of relationship, wouldn't just be dangerous on an emotional level when it ended—which of course it would—it could complicate his relationship with Nico, which would be so much worse.

Nico needed this man in his life and she suspected that, despite all his protestations to the contrary, Lukas was just beginning to discover how much he needed Nico too. Even if she had been bold enough, and secure enough, to risk an affair with Lukas, she would never forgive herself if something she did threatened the bond he was just beginning to form with his nephew.

'That's bull and you know it,' he said, slicing off her argument at the knees. 'One thing has nothing to do with the other.'

'Of course it does,' she said, finally locating the indignation she'd been searching for at his dismissive reply. 'I want to nurture and support your relationship with him,' she added. 'And I can't do that if we're involved.'

'Why not?' he asked, not looking conflicted in the slightest.

'Because I live here, with him.'

'So what?'

'I don't want him to know that there's…' She stammered to a halt, his blank expression unnerving her even more. 'That there's something going on between us. He might think you're coming here to see me instead of him.'

'He's four,' he said flatly.

'Nico's very smart and intuitive,' she said, feeling as if she were under siege.

'I know that,' he said. 'He's also confident and well-adjusted. And he seems to have a pretty healthy ego. So there's no reason on earth why he should question my motives for coming to see him. But anyway, Nico's reaction is irrelevant. Because he's not going to find out that we're sleeping together.'

'How could he not?' she said.

'Because I'm buying a place for you where we can meet a couple of evenings a week,' he said, shocking her into silence. 'I'm already paying Maureen a hefty salary so we might as well get her to earn it.'

'Whoa! Wait.' She reared back, his astonishing arrogance appalling her, and giving her the power to resist the heat sizzling over her skin. 'I haven't agreed to any of this,' she said. 'I don't want you to buy me a place. And I don't want to become your...' She searched frantically for the correct word. 'Your... Your mistress.'

The term sounded antiquated, but it bolstered her temper and gave her the ammunition she needed in the battle with her feelings towards him.

Maybe Lukas had secrets about why he had been so desperate not to bond with Nico, but he was still an arrogant, entitled... How dare he expect her to prioritise a sexual relationship with him over Nico's needs?

'Nico needs me. I won't be your kept woman, and I don't want to be.'

Lukas was so annoyed he could hardly see straight, let alone think, because he'd been balancing on a knife-edge of desire for several hours now. Every time their eyes connected, every time he noticed that spark of approval, the glow of warmth in her expression, it had made the flash fire of his temper more intense.

'I'm already paying for everything,' he barked, the words spewing out on a wave of frustration. 'What the heck difference does it make if we both get some fun out of the deal?'

The second the words left his lips he wanted to grab them back, because the defiance in her eyes turned to shocked outrage.

'You bastard.' Tears misted her eyes but refused to fall. 'I'm not for sale. I accepted your financial help for Nico's sake. But I don't need it. He doesn't need it. We were surviving perfectly well on our own. If the price of staying here is sleeping with you, we'll leave.'

Damn it. That was not what he had meant at all.

What they'd shared last night had nothing whatsoever to do with his responsibilities towards the boy—and her. But the threat to leave was like pouring accelerant on an already smouldering fire.

He'd sworn to keep the boy safe, to protect him. He was not about to let her take him—or herself—anywhere.

'You attempt to move Nico out of here and I'll haul you up in court quicker than you can say *child custody battle.*'

'You can't take him away from me—I'm his guardian,' she said, but all he could see was the dark dilated pupils, the passion she was continuing to deny, the ragged rise and fall of those full breasts—and all he could think about was the way she'd messed him around today, using the boy as a shield.

'Try me,' he said.

'I hate you,' she declared.

'No, you don't.' Suddenly, the need he'd always kept

on lockdown, had always been able to qualify and control, broke through like a dam bursting its banks.

He hauled her into his arms.

To hell with this. He was through pretending that last night hadn't been good, hadn't been glorious. Or that it wasn't going to happen again.

He pressed his lips to the pulse in her neck, felt it flutter beneath his tongue. She jerked in his arms but didn't draw back, her palms flattening on his waist, her fingers fisting in his sweater as he worked his way to her mouth.

Her lips parted on a shattered gasp and he sank into the kiss, his tongue thrusting deep. He explored, feeding the swell of emotion in his chest and feasting on the hunger between them. The hunger which had been unleashed last night but which he'd seen so clearly in her eyes every time she'd looked at him today. His fingers tangled in her hair, angling her head back as he felt the shudder of a response she couldn't control. The hunger intensified as she kissed him back, her tongue dancing with his in an elemental rhythm.

He tore his mouth away first, her body limp and pliant in his arms.

Her cheeks were blazing, her full lips were reddened from the fury of the kiss—but as the desire cleared, her eyes became pools of shock and anguish.

He released her and she stumbled back. He should have been satisfied, her instinctive response a vindication. But instead he felt unsteady on his feet and shocked right down to his core at what he had done.

What the heck had just happened?

He'd never kissed a woman in anger before. Never allowed his need to show. And never been so affected by her response.

'I'm going to be away for two weeks. When I come back we are going to discuss this again. Like adults.' He ground the words out, trying to regain control, not just of her and this situation but of himself.

He wasn't an animal. And he never let his temper get the better of him, but somehow he had with her.

She remained mute, her hand covering her mouth, her eyes widening. Reminding him, as if he needed any reminding, of how inexperienced she was.

'What happens between the two of us has nothing to do with Nico or my relationship with him,' he said, trying to repair the damage he'd done with that knee-jerk threat to take her to court for the boy's custody.

She just stared back at him, the emotions crossing her face—shame, concern, panic—so transparent it only made her more vulnerable.

His phone vibrated in his pocket and he tugged it out.

It took him a moment to register the flight reminder that flashed up on the screen.

'I need to leave.' He shoved his phone back into his pocket. He didn't care about the damn flight. He'd probably missed it already. But he needed to take this opportunity to retreat and regroup.

He was behaving like a lunatic—a man he didn't even recognise. Threatening Bronte, however unintentionally, or kissing her into submission wasn't the answer. All it would do was inflame the situation, bringing volatile emotions into something that was nothing more than a strong sexual connection.

The look of relief on her face made him more aware of just how badly he'd messed up.

'As soon as I'm back in the country,' he added, trying to keep his voice even, the tone pragmatic, 'I'll send a car to get you, so we can continue this conversation in private.' By which time he would be in complete control of his faculties again—if it killed him.

'I'm not one of your employees, Lukas,' she said, finally finding her voice.

'Don't I know it,' he muttered as he walked past her to grasp the door handle. 'Two weeks.'

The sparkle of temper in her eyes at his ultimatum was an improvement on the wary shock of moments before. So he'd take it.

He walked out of the room, refusing to look back. But as he made his way down the stairs his pulse pounded in his ears almost as violently as the heat firing through his veins from their aborted kiss.

He had two long weeks to get a grip before he saw her again.

But as he settled into the chauffeur-driven car parked outside the mews entrance the desire pooling in his groin became painful. He shifted in his seat. The dumb decision to kiss her hadn't just hoisted him by his own petard; it might very well cripple him too.

CHAPTER SEVEN

BRONTE WATCHED AS the pink lines in the window of the pregnancy testing kit thickened and spread, like the anacondas writhing in her stomach and tightening around her throat.

It can't be right. It just can't.

She shook the white plastic stick frantically, but the two thick pink lines refused to disappear.

Collapsing onto the toilet seat, she fumbled one-handed with the instruction leaflet and scanned it again. Looking for an out. A reinterpretation that wouldn't force her to face the truth.

She was pregnant. With Lukas Blackstone's child.

No. No. No.

She'd taken the test as a precaution, sure she was overreacting, convinced it was just a formality. That she couldn't possibly have fallen pregnant.

She'd been trying not to think about Lukas and everything that had happened two weeks ago—her emotions had been in turmoil for days after his visit. She'd hardly slept. So she'd made a concerted effort to put him, and his ultimatum, the kiss she'd been unable to resist and his threat to take Nico away from her out of her mind. But this morning she'd received a text from Lisa informing her that Lukas's car would be arriving to pick her up at four o'clock—and it was only then that she'd realised it was two weeks since she'd seen Lukas. And slept with him. And she hadn't had a period.

Standing on shaky legs, forcing herself to breathe, she dumped the test in the bathroom bin and stared at her face in the mirror.

So what are you going to do now?

She'd been in denial about what had happened in his penthouse, refused to deal with any of it. And now her situation was about a billion times worse.

Running away from your problems never solved anything.

When exactly had she lost sight of that, as well as everything else—her common sense, her practicality, her sense of self-worth?

He'd dragged her into his arms, pressed his face into her neck, made her feel needed, wanted, important, desired. And she'd responded, instantly and unequivocally. She'd kissed him back, letting her own needs consume her, despite his ruthless threat to take Nico from her, despite his arrogant demand that she become his mistress.

She touched a hand to her abdomen, panic and fear churning in her stomach and sending the writhing snakes into the pit of her belly... Or maybe it was the first sign of morning sickness.

A termination, of course, was the sensible answer. And the answer that Lukas would no doubt suggest. He might even try to insist upon it. But even the thought made the bile rise up in her throat and threaten to gag her.

Her hand pressed into her flat stomach.

She couldn't have this baby. She didn't even want to tell Lukas about it. If he'd been pushy and domineering up to now, surely he would be even more so when he found out how stupid she'd been. And that she'd lied to him.

Not only that, but what about Nico? He was her first priority. Would this give Lukas even more ammunition to have her declared an unfit guardian?

The memory of Lukas's face, shocked and wary, and the way his whole body had stiffened when Nico had charged towards him on his visit two weeks ago spun through her mind and taunted her. As she recalled how he had changed during the course of the morning, how he'd made a concerted effort to talk to the boy, to communicate with him on a level he understood. How he'd reached out in that one unguarded moment and stroked Nico's hair.

She had to be realistic. Lukas wouldn't want this child. Maybe he had reluctantly begun to bond with Nico. As an uncle. But he'd made it very clear he did not want to be a father.

He would be furious at this turn of events. And while she wasn't scared of his temper, she was terrified of wanting to ask something of him that he was incapable of giving.

Her hand trembled as she caressed the non-existent bump.

But, even knowing that, she knew she couldn't have a termination. Because, however big a mistake this pregnancy was, however unforeseen and catastrophic, however much it would complicate her life and Nico's and even Lukas's, it already felt like more than just a problem that needed to be solved.

The soft knock on the bathroom door startled Bronte.

'Bronte, a car has arrived to take you to Mr Blackstone's hotel,' Maureen's soft voice came through the wood.

Panic and an unwanted desire—the same unwanted

desire that had been tearing her apart for the last two weeks as she waited for Lukas's return—coalesced in the pit of her stomach and churned like a perfect storm, spreading heat and horrified yearning over the snakes writhing in her belly.

She switched off the tap and dabbed the heat blazing in her cheeks with a towel, while also attempting to damp down the hysteria rising up her throat.

She would have to tell Lukas about the baby.

She dropped the towel, a thought skidding into her fevered mind that seemed grimly fortuitous. At least the news of this pregnancy would solve one problem. He would have no desire to pursue a relationship with her now. So she wouldn't have to worry about her kamikaze reaction to his kisses any more.

'Tell them I'll be down in a minute,' she murmured.

Despite all her frantic qualifications though, as she walked down the stairs towards the mansion's back entrance and bid goodbye to Maureen, the hot snakes in her stomach hissed... And she didn't feel anywhere near as relieved as she should.

Anticipation and frustration washed through Lukas as the elevator bell pinged in his penthouse. He turned from his contemplation of the afternoon traffic on Park Lane to see the bodyguard he'd sent to accompany Bronte step out.

The tight knots in his shoulder blades released as the bulky man held the door open and Bronte followed him out of the elevator.

Her head rose as he walked towards her, trying to keep his steps even and slow.

'Hello, Bronte. Thank you for coming,' he said. She was stunningly beautiful, those wide tilted eyes mossy green pools of emotion.

The flare of desire was sharp and swift and all-consuming. He shoved his fists into the pockets of his pants to stop himself from reaching out and dragging her into his arms.

He'd had fourteen sleepless nights since he'd last seen her, and he still hadn't got a handle on the effect she had on him.

She wore her trademark tomboy attire of well-worn jeans and a tank top and checked shirt. If she was trying to disguise her lush curves though, or the appeal of that supple, responsive body, she was failing.

'I didn't think I had a choice,' she replied, but the flash of defiance he had hoped for wasn't there.

He nodded to the security guard, who disappeared back into the elevator. He didn't want an audience for what he had to say next.

He hadn't been able to stop thinking about Bronte. About the things they'd done together the last time she had come to him here. And the way he'd behaved the morning after. It seemed she hadn't forgotten either from the bright flush on her cheeks, or the wary watchfulness in those expressive eyes.

'You did have a choice,' he said, determined to make amends. 'I'm sorry; I didn't make that clear.'

He'd gone over their parting words, and that brutal parting kiss, a million times in his head. And there was no way of getting around it. He'd behaved like a prize jerk. That she turned him on to the point of madness wasn't an excuse.

She'd been innocent, inexperienced. A virgin, for goodness' sake. Initiating virgins wasn't something he'd had any experience of. But that was no excuse either. He should have been careful with her, gentle, persuasive—not pounced on her like a starving man. If he had been struggling to control the strength of his attraction to her, the hunger that had consumed him then and was consuming him now, how the heck did he expect her to deal with it? Other than to try and shut it down?

He was going to have to pay a penance now. And make the effort to show her that an affair could be good for both of them. It was a new experience for him, having to disguise the strength of his attraction to a woman. Mostly because he'd never been as attracted to any woman as he was to this one. Before now, if things weren't working out he'd always been able to walk away. He didn't pressure women into sex, and he'd never had a mistress either. But he wanted that security and stability with Bronte. He already knew his thirst for her wasn't going to be easily quenched. Not least because it wasn't just the sex that captivated him, but so many other things about her. Her fierce loyalty to Nico. Her determination to maintain her independence. Her refreshing honesty and the myriad emotions he could read so easily on her open, extraordinary face—despite her best efforts to hide them.

She wasn't doing a lot to hide them now, he noted. She looked tense and anxious. And unfortunately there was no point in deluding himself any longer. He was the cause.

'Come and sit down so we can discuss this situation rationally.' He swept his hand towards the couches facing the panoramic view of Hyde Park.

'I'd rather stand,' she said, her stance stiff and uncomfortable. She folded her arms around her midriff in a protective gesture that had a novel feeling engulfing him.

Guilt.

'Are you scared of me, Bronte?' he asked.

Those deep emerald eyes flashed to his and he saw surprise. *Thank God.*

'No, of course not,' she said, seeming genuinely per-plexed and even a little guilty. Even if she didn't have a damn thing to be guilty about. Unlike him.

Time to own it, Blackstone, and then start working on that charm offensive you've been planning for two solid weeks.

'Good,' he said. 'Then sit down and I'll get you a drink.' He strode to the bar, grateful to have something to do with his hands.

This was a novel experience for him too, he realised. He'd never had to work to get a woman into his bed be-fore now. Which was probably why he'd made such a monumental mess of this seduction two weeks ago. Let-ting his temper and his sexual frustration blind him to her needs, her nerves and her inexperience. That wasn't going to happen again.

'What would you like?' he asked, pouring himself a glass of bourbon. Another first, he thought, as he downed the stiff drink in one and the shot of fire burned his throat to warm his belly.

He didn't usually drink hard liquor, and certainly not while with a woman. He preferred to keep his instincts sharp. But right now dulling them wouldn't be a bad move; his instincts were sharper than they needed to be with this woman. He had to take this slow and easy. He couldn't risk scaring her off again. Or he might never get what he wanted. What they both wanted.

'Wine? Beer? Something stronger?' he asked when she didn't reply.

The guilty flush spread up to her hairline. 'Um... something soft, please. Water?'

He nodded and selected a bottle of Scottish mineral water from the fridge. He unscrewed the top, popped it in the trash and then poured the liquid into a glass. Taking his time, he sat in the seat opposite her and handed her the glass.

Their fingertips brushed and he felt a jolt. She jerked her hand away, sloshing water over her wrist, then took a hasty gulp.

He had to hold back a smile.

Good to know.

She still felt it too. The desire which was already tying his guts in knots. All he had to do was show her that what she felt for him didn't have to be dangerous or complicated. It was simply a strong biological connection.

He knew that, she didn't, because she'd never had this connection with anyone else. Well, hell, neither had he. Nothing this strong anyway. But at least he knew how to handle it. And how much pleasure they could get out of it. But first he had to dismantle the defences she'd erected— then prove to her what he was proposing was a great deal more flexible than he'd let her believe.

He watched her drink the water, the sight of her throat working as she swallowed sending another jolt of lust to his groin—which was probably perverse, but everything about this woman turned him on.

'I have a proposition for you,' he said.

Her eyes flashed to his, igniting his senses even more.

'I can't be your mistress,' she said, her distress all too obvious from the hectic colour staining her cheekbones. But her choice of words—*can't*, not *don't want to be*—gave him an opening. An opening he intended to exploit if he could.

'And I can't stop you from threatening to take Nico away from me either,' she said, blinking furiously. 'But I have something to....'

'Bronte, don't say any more.' He cut her off, the renewed wave of guilt unprecedented as he caught the sheen of moisture in her eyes. 'You misunderstood me. I didn't threaten to sue for custody of Nico because I wanted you to sleep with me.'

Damn, he had really screwed this up.

'Then why did you say it?' she asked, not looking convinced.

'I panicked,' he admitted, feeling like a fool.

'I don't understand,' she said, as forthright as always. 'What did you panic about?'

Leaning forward, he threaded his fingers together, not quite able to look at her as he was forced to break his golden rule and explain himself.

'You threatened to remove him and yourself from the house in Regent's Park. I can't let you do that. But whether or not you were willing to sleep with me had no bearing on that.'

'Why can't you *let* me?' she asked without a hint of sarcasm.

He sighed, knowing he would be forced to reveal something only a handful of people knew. Something he had never wanted anyone to know.

'When I was seven years old I was kidnapped,' he said. Ignoring her sudden gasp, he made himself continue. 'They were a ruthless criminal gang. They snatched me in Central Park, while I was there with Alexei and our governess. They'd been planning it for months. They kept me for three days, while they tried to persuade my father to pay a million-dollar ransom.' He rubbed his thumb over the scar on his cheek as the memory of the rending pain, the childish terror, bombarded him.

'The scar? They cut you?' Bronte's eyes widened with horror and something a great deal more disturbing. Compassion. 'It wasn't an accident?'

He let his thumb drop, disturbed by her intuition and

her reaction to the news. 'That's not relevant,' he quali-fied quickly because she looked devastated by his rev-elation. And the one thing he didn't need from her was her pity. 'The point is, they would have killed me, were preparing to kill me, when I was rescued by the SWAT team. I was lucky to survive. I'm not prepared to put your life or Nico's life at risk in that way because of your as-sociation with me. Which means you have to stay where I can keep you safe. Now do you understand?'

Bronte nodded, the power of speech having deserted her. He looked so indomitable, his expression rigidly con-trolled. But she'd seen the flicker of something raw and so painful in his expression when he'd rubbed the jag-ged scar—that the horrifying thought of him as a child, being brutalised in that way for money, had felt like being stabbed in the stomach.

'Okay,' she managed at last because he seemed to need an answer.

There were so many more questions she wanted to ask him. How had he survived? Not just the pain, but the fear? Three days would be an eternity to a child. Was that why he kept his emotions under such ruthless control? Why he'd struggled with making an attachment to Nico? Surely a trauma of that magnitude at such an impression-able age would have a devastating effect on any person.

She stopped herself from asking him any of those questions, though. Because she doubted he would answer them. His closed expression suggested that even giving her this much information about the incident had been a struggle for him.

But compassion for that little boy, and the man he had become, swamped her regardless. And tangled with the guilty knowledge of her pregnancy.

She should have told him about the baby as soon as she'd arrived. She'd intended to, but seeing him again had been so overwhelming she'd needed to compose herself, to figure out exactly how to say it. And when she'd finally worked up the guts to do it he'd interrupted her. And then given her this devastating glimpse of the trauma he'd suffered during his childhood—his tone so controlled and unemotional it had broken her heart. As if sharing the pain of those moments would somehow diminish him in her eyes.

Consequently, the news of her pregnancy was now lodged in her throat like a boulder that she couldn't seem to expel. Suddenly his motives two weeks ago—when he'd told her he didn't have it in him to be a father, that he didn't make *love*, that he didn't need love—seemed so much more complex.

What if he'd said that, what if he believed it, not because he was cold and emotionless but because he needed to believe it to protect himself? If she told him about the baby now, he would react the only way he knew how, the way he'd done as that traumatised child. By shutting down his emotions and denying they existed. He'd feel threatened and trapped again, and he would have every right to feel that way because she'd lied to him.

Telling him the truth now would destroy this *thing* between them before it had ever had a chance to grow.

Would it be so wrong to give it a chance, not just for her own sake but for their child's?

'The proposition I'm going to make would always be based on mutual consent,' he said. 'Believe me, I'm not going to threaten or bully you into my bed. If you're not there of your own free will it would destroy my pleasure just as much as yours.'

She managed a mute nod again, heat flooding through

her at the intensity in his gaze. And the memory of his hands on her hips, his huge erection seated deep inside her. Perhaps the connection they had was purely sexual. But would it be so wrong to discover if it could be more than that?

'But I'm not going to deny I want you back in my bed,' he added. 'Any way I can get you. I've had sex with a lot of women, Bronte. I've got a healthy sex drive, probably above average, but even so I've never wanted a woman the way I want you.'

It wasn't a declaration of his feelings. He was talking about the sexual chemistry between them. She knew that, but even so she felt the deep tug of yearning twist and turn inside her and morph into something that felt like hope.

'I'd very much like to explore that connection,' he continued, his voice so husky now it seemed to scrape over her nerve endings like sandpaper, igniting and agitating every inch of her skin. 'I know you're inexperienced so I'm prepared to take it slow. I'm not great at compromise but we can negotiate the where and when and how of this liaison. I want you to be comfortable. But I think it would be madness not to make the most of a physical connection that has the potential to give us both so much pleasure. Don't you?'

It was a direct question. One which she should only have one answer to. No.

Sleeping with Lukas Blackstone again was the height of insanity—from an emotional point of view. A leap of faith that she had promised herself she would never make again, ever since she'd been a little girl and she'd stood on her father's doorstep praying for him to look at her, just once.

But even before she'd taken the pregnancy test this morning she'd known, although she had refused to admit it to herself, she was already more invested, more drawn to Lukas than she should be. And despite the deep throbbing in her sex, the dizzying, disorientating rush of adrenaline at Lukas's proposition, she knew that investment had always been more than just physical.

Surely now though, after what she had discovered less than an hour ago, she had the incentive to discover how much more.

She was pregnant with Lukas's child. Whatever happened now, she would always have a connection to this man. Would it be so terribly wrong to take this opportunity to get to know him better? Before she told him about the pregnancy?

Even with her tiny amount of experience, she knew it was a massive mistake to think sex with Lukas would lead to emotional intimacy—especially as she now knew why he was so guarded. But surely physical closeness—and spending time with him—would give her the opportunity to at least answer some of the many questions she had about him. Didn't she deserve to know those answers?

And then there was all the pleasure he was promising too. She'd never regretted the sacrifices she'd made to look after Nikky, because the rewards had been astronomical—not just in every smile and cuddle she got from him, but also in the things she'd discovered about herself as a person. But what was wrong with wanting to experience more of the wild, uninhibited joy she had found in Lukas Blackstone's arms? Why should she feel guilty about wanting him?

She clasped her hands in her lap and stared out of the window of his penthouse. She took a deep breath and turned back to him, to see the inscrutable concentration on his face. Excitement and terror surged.

Be brave. Take a chance.

'Okay,' she murmured, her breath choking out.

His eyebrows rose, the evidence that he hadn't been 100 per cent sure of her answer making her even more sure of her decision. Maybe he wasn't quite as arrogant as he seemed either.

'You're sure?' he asked.

She nodded.

He stood and stepped over the coffee table, then grasped her trembling fingers in one firm hand and tugged her to her feet. He cupped her cheek, let his fingers delve into her hair as he angled her head for his mouth, then stopped inches from completing the kiss she already yearned for beyond reason.

'You need to say the words, Bronte, before I can kiss you,' he commanded softly.

She felt a smile curve her lips, tremulous, determined and only slightly terrified.

'Are you going to keep telling me what to do? Because if you are, I may change my mind,' she found herself saying, not sure where the strength to tease him came from, but impossibly pleased with the result when his lips drew another millimetre closer.

'No, you won't,' he said, the smile in his voice impossibly alluring. 'Because I won't let you.'

She had only a moment to gasp in mock outrage before his mouth was on hers—taking, demanding, tempting. The rich taste of the bourbon shattered the last of her defences as he licked across the seam of her lips. She kissed him back, letting the excitement surge as he explored her mouth in masterful strokes.

She swayed and firm hands gripped her waist, holding her steady as his lips travelled down to the pulse point in her neck to nip and suck and drive her wild.

She was panting, breathing so heavily she was scared

she might start to hyperventilate, as his hands travelled up her back, gliding under the soft cotton of her camisole. His thumbs toyed with the peaks of her breasts, the nipples tightening into throbbing points even through the fabric of her bra. She arched into the caress, desperate to feel his touch on naked flesh, annoyed by the clothes inhibiting them.

'Please, I… Can you take off my bra?' she stammered, the colour flooding her cheeks when he drew back and her whole body shuddered in protest—and unrequited need.

Dropping his hands from her breasts, he cupped her cheeks.

Humiliation swept through her when a smile tugged at those firm sensual lips. Had she actually just begged him to take off her bra?

'I'm sorry, I didn't mean to give you orders.' Or sound so desperate, she thought when his smile became more pronounced.

He chuckled, the sound rusty. 'You don't have to apologise for telling me what you want.'

'Oh… Well, good,' she said, feeling ridiculous. Insecurity flooded her. 'But why did you stop then?'

His dark eyes flashed with a fire so intense she felt scalded.

'I'm not stopping, but how about we slow down?'

She wasn't sure it was a question but she nodded anyway, mesmerised by the gruff note of need. She hadn't turned him off. This was good.

He lifted her hand to his lips then kissed the knuckles, and each of her fingers in turn. The act was tender, reverential, but also carnal. Her heart lurched in her chest as heat bloomed in her abdomen.

He laved the webbing between her fingers, mapped

the tracery of veins on the back of her hand, tested the swell of flesh beneath her thumb with his teeth and finally planted his lips on the pulse point pounding in her wrist.

She gasped and squirmed as the shock wave of sensation speared through her body.

Who knew her hand was an erogenous zone?

Grasping her fingers—limp now with desire—he tugged her against him and wrapped her hand around his back until her whole body softened against the hard lines of his. The powerful jut of his erection, outlined against her stomach, sent a quiver of reaction arrowing down.

'FYI,' he whispered against her hair, tracing the shell of her ear with that deviously coaxing tongue, 'you couldn't turn me off if you tried.'

She leaned back, a little horrified that he had been able to read her doubts so easily. But what she saw in his face—the rigid control, accompanied by wry amusement and unadulterated need—sent a betraying shudder of excitement through her.

You're not lying to him about the baby...you're simply delaying telling him the truth.

Clasping her hand, he led her towards the bedroom suite, which was flooded with natural light from the late autumn sunset.

'Could we close the blinds?' she said as he closed the door behind them.

He cradled her cheek, a wry smile reaching his eyes. 'The windows are treated; no one can see in. And anyway, we're thirty-one floors up.'

'It's not that.'

His brows lifted in quizzical enquiry, forcing her to spell it out.

'Last time we did this it was darker.' And she'd had a lot less to hide. 'I'm not used to men…to anyone seeing me naked.'

The unfamiliar pang of tenderness struck Lukas—not just at her request, which made him all the more aware of her inexperience—but at the bravery with which she delivered it, despite the quiver of uncertainty.

Damn, what the hell am I going to do with you, Bronte?

She was so much more than he had expected. And so much sweeter, and hotter, and more straightforward than he was used to.

Which made her vulnerable in ways he had never considered.

He'd accepted he would have to be careful with her, that he would have to keep his more basic and elemental desires on lockdown until she got used to being in his bed. Which was why he hadn't given into the desire to rip her clothes off the minute she'd asked. But until this moment he hadn't considered anything beyond their sexual connection. She'd been so strong and independent up till now, it hadn't even occurred to him that the responsibility not to hurt her, not to take too much, went way beyond the physical.

The thought disturbed him. He'd never had this responsibility before, never wanted it.

But, unfortunately, as she stood before him and he noticed for the first time how slender she was, how small and fragile compared to him, he knew backing away now wasn't an option. The ache in his groin spiked, as if to remind him and get his libido back on track.

He quelled the desire to suggest they keep the shades up just because he wanted to see every inch of her succulent flesh while he devoured it.

He fished his cell phone out of his pocket and opened the app which controlled the apartment's electronics. Then adjusted the shades. The glow of the setting sun dimmed but did nothing to take away the golden quality of the light on her skin. Not quite ready to give up the game completely, he brought the lights up a fraction because while he was willing to make adjustments for her shyness, he wasn't about to make love to her in the dark. The concession felt worth it though, when the rigid line of her shoulders relaxed.

'Okay?' he asked as he flung his phone on the dresser.

'Yes, thank you,' she said, and he couldn't help it, he laughed, breaking at least a little of the tension mounting in the room, her studied politeness striking him as comical.

'Did I say something funny?' she said, dismayed.

He placed a hand on her butt to anchor her to him and chuckled again. That had to be another first, he thought vaguely. He couldn't remember the last time he'd laughed during sex. Sex was usually a serious business for him—a bargain struck between two consenting adults to achieve sexual satisfaction—but with her it felt spontaneous, joyful, fun in a way it never had before.

'No,' he said as he concentrated on unbuttoning her shirt and dragging it off her shoulders.

'Then why are you laughing?' she said, sounding a little defensive.

The shirt dropped to the floor and he sobered, the rush of heat obliterating everything else. The stiff peaks of her breasts were clearly visible through her tank and bra, her breaths making her curves more abundant.

He moistened his lips, the desire to feel those ripe nipples stiffen against his tongue drying his mouth. Hooking his forefinger into the belt of her jeans, he tugged her closer, close enough to strip off the tank and release the hook on her bra.

'I'm not laughing any more,' he murmured, breaking the strained silence as he dragged down the thick cotton straps, discarded the bra and cupped the heavy flesh in his palms.

He rubbed his thumbs over the resilient peaks then plucked and played, learning the shape and texture of her and gauging her reaction. He revelled in her unguarded response, the broken sobs as her nipples swelled and hardened.

Her eyes glazed with stunned passion, her back arching in instinctive invitation. He bent to drag one straining tip into his mouth.

She pushed into his mouth as he feasted on the sweet taste of her desperation. His fingers became urgent as he fumbled with her belt, popped open the buttons on her fly and eased her jeans over slim hips.

She held his head, her fingers gripping his hair as he continued the sharp suction on her breast and pressed the heel of his palm to her core over damp cotton. She bucked against his hold but he ignored her startled breath, the sultry spice of her arousal filling his nostrils as he slid his fingers beneath her panties and found the plump, swollen folds of her sex.

She was soaking wet, his fingers gliding against the stiff button of her clitoris with ease.

He stroked over it and around it, teasing her, testing her, her shuddering response as she charged towards orgasm making his erection strain so hard against his fly he was surprised it didn't rip open his pants.

'Oh…oh,' she sobbed incoherently against his ear. 'I can't…'

'Yes, you can,' he demanded, stroking ruthlessly

now—desperate to see her shatter. Thrusting one finger then two into the tight clasp of her body, he massaged the walls of her sex.

She cried out against his ear, her body gripping his fingers as he thrust her into orgasm. His own climax licked at his spine. She collapsed against him, limp and sated and all his.

Scooping her into his arms, he strode to the bed but the weirdest thought assailed him as he stripped off her pants and boots, tugged down her panties and then tore off his own clothes and fumbled with the condom.

If he didn't get inside her in the next ten seconds, burying himself so deep that he was the only thing she could think about or feel, he might very well die.

CHAPTER EIGHT

'THE HORMONE LEVELS in your test are consistent with your dates, which makes you six weeks' gestation. So if you're considering termination I'd strongly recommend that you make the decision soon.' The young female nurse sent Bronte a fleeting smile tinged with sympathy.

'I'm not,' Bronte said, her hand straying back to the life growing in her belly.

'Is there anything else you want to ask me?' the nurse said gently. 'You can still take more time to think about the options if you need to.'

Bronte shook her head. 'I don't need time to think about it. I've decided I want to have the baby.' The words came out on a whisper of breath, the first time she'd ever said them out loud. But all the reasons why having this baby would be a disaster didn't hijack the bubble of happiness sitting under her breastbone.

She would have to tell Lukas now. She couldn't keep it a secret any longer. She'd started feeling nauseous some mornings and it had been a month since they'd started sleeping together regularly—hot, feral, erotic encounters snatched whenever she was willing to go to his penthouse. She'd limited those encounters to two days a week, and made sure that she never stayed with him overnight, to at least try to keep her emotions in perspective.

But the more time she spent with Lukas, the more desperate she became to crack the shell he kept around his feelings. Because over the evenings they'd shared together her own shell had crumbled. Every time he stroked or licked or thrust her to orgasm, every time he held her afterwards and tried to cajole her to stay, she'd become convinced the connection they shared went way beyond the sex.

The way he insisted on accompanying her back to the house whenever they had a liaison. The fact he hadn't left the country since she'd agreed to their arrangement. The way he called her every day. And the effort he was making to forge a relationship with Nico.

She'd even begun to see those increasingly autocratic texts, when he demanded to know if she would be visiting the penthouse that evening, as a sign of his deepening need for her in his life, rather than just a sign that he was far too used to getting his own way.

Bronte's mind continued to mull over all the possibilities as the nurse handed her some pamphlets about antenatal care, gave her the contact information for the local antenatal group and a referral notice for a local GP.

She stuffed the information in her bag as she left the clinic, and walked back through the bustling streets of Camden on a Monday afternoon. The thought of the conversation she must have with Lukas the next time they met had anxiety strangling the bubble of hope a little. His thoughts and feelings about her and the course of their relationship—other than how much he enjoyed igniting her senses to fever-pitch—still remained a secret in many ways. She hadn't expected him to make a commitment so soon, but she had hoped that he might have been willing to confide in her a bit more.

She'd tried to probe about the kidnapping, tried to

discover how he felt about Nico's increasing attachment to him—which was bordering on full-blown hero-worship since Lukas had arrived unannounced to spend the afternoon the day before teaching the little boy how to throw a baseball—but he either derailed the conversation or distracted her with sex.

As she turned into Regent's Crescent, she lifted the collar of her coat and put on her sunglasses despite the weak winter sunlight filtering through the trees. There were very few paparazzi around these days, and she'd taken precautions this morning to leave early to get to her clinic appointment but, even so, she checked her surroundings before slipping into the back alleyway that led to the mews behind her home.

The persistent buzz of her mobile phone stopped her in her tracks. The little bubble of hope expanded when she read the caller ID: *Lukas mobile.*

Entering the back garden, she answered the call. 'Hey.'

'Hey, yourself—where have you been?' came the curt reply. 'I just spoke to Maureen and she said you left the house this morning without a bodyguard.'

Guilt coalesced in her stomach. 'I went for a walk,' she murmured.

She would have to tell Lukas today, but she didn't want to tell him over the phone. She needed to speak to him face to face—she still had no idea what his reaction would be to news of the baby. But what scared her most of all was how emotionally invested she had become in his response. If the news ended their affair she would have to deal with it. But if he rejected her and the baby it would be much harder to handle than it would have been four weeks ago, before she'd agreed to his proposition. Because now she had comprehensive proof that this autocratic, demanding, arrogant man also had the ability to be so tender, so protective, so caring.

'Where are you now?' he demanded, sounding more annoyed than tender.

'I'm almost home.'

'Almost home where, exactly?'

'In the back garden,' she said, locking the gate behind her.

She heard a muffled curse then a heavy sigh down the other end of the line.

'Dammit, Bronte. How many times do I have to tell you? I don't want you or Nico taking those kinds of risks. If you want to go for a walk, fine. But I expect you to take the proper precautions, which means having James or Janice or one of the other bodyguards with you at all times when you're out of the house.'

Bronte supposed she ought to be at least a little indignant at his high-handed attitude, but all she could hear was his concern. And all she could think about was him as a child, torn from everything he knew for three horrifying days.

'I never go out with Nico without protection,' she managed in her defence, as guilt blossomed under her breastbone like a rash. She hadn't taken James with her this time because she hadn't wanted him to report back to Lukas where she was going.

When exactly had her altruistic reasons for keeping the baby a secret begun to feel dishonest and selfish?

She should have told him much sooner. She'd never intended to keep it a secret this long. But being with him had been so seductive. Not just the sex, but all those moments too when she would lie in his arms and he would ask her about Nico or they would chat about the new resort. It had seemed so normal, so different and new to have someone else to chat to about things that had once been her responsibility alone. To share details of her day—and the burden of bringing up a rambunctious little boy with someone else who had a connection to him. And to have him share details of his day with her—which appeared to involve endless meetings and high pressure decisions.

The wonder of having that companionship with a man as dynamic and charismatic as Lukas had made it that much easier for her to come up with excuses not to tell him about the baby, and risk jeopardising that closeness, that connection.

There was a long pause on the other end of the line. 'Nico's safety isn't the only thing that matters to me,' he said, his voice so gruff it was as if the comment had been wrenched from him.

It was hardly an admission of undying love, but still Bronte's heart expanded, all the hopes and dreams she'd tried not to give free rein to galloping out of hiding.

'Okay,' she murmured, her throat closing.

She heard his strained chuckle.

'Seriously?' he said, his surprise evident. 'No arguments about your independence?'

A smile edged her lips at the husky tone. 'Not today.'

'Good,' he said, his voice becoming huskier. 'But just so you know, next time you pull a stunt like this, I'm prepared to tie you to the bed to make you behave yourself.' She could hear the smile in his voice and knew he was joking… Mostly. But still the tug of heat in her abdomen became a definite yank and the swell of emotion in her throat surged.

'I'd like to see you try,' she said, teasing him back in an attempt to slow her galloping heartbeat.

'Don't tempt me,' he said. Then added, 'I want to see you this afternoon.'

'I'm coming over tonight,' she reminded him, her anxiety resurfacing in a rush. They'd arranged their 'playdate' yesterday, after he'd spent the afternoon with Nico. But once she told him about the baby, would it be their last?

'I don't want to wait that long,' he said.

She glanced at the clock on her phone, the tangle of emotions—desire, anxiety, tenderness and, worst of all, that unbridled hope—starting to crucify her.

'It's only four hours,' she said. 'I can't come any sooner. I have to get Nico settled for the night before I can leave.' It wasn't entirely true. Nico was more than happy to have Maureen put him to bed, but Bronte had maintained the night-time ritual ever since she'd started her affair with Lukas. Partly because she had always loved those moments before bedtime with Nico—the feel of his sturdy young body, so healthy now, snuggled under her arm. But as she heard Lukas's heartfelt groan she admitted that wasn't the only reason why she'd refused to go to Lukas's penthouse before Nico went to bed each night.

As the effects of her pregnancy had started to show— the swelling in her breasts, the tiredness, especially after they made love—she'd been that much more aware of how much she wanted to make them a family. Her, Lukas, Nico and the new baby. And it had been harder and harder for her not to give in to the hope.

'So I'm being thrown over for a four-year-old,' he murmured. 'Way to shoot down a guy's ego.'

'I'm sure your ego will survive,' she said as she knocked on the back door.

He barked out a strained laugh as Maureen opened the door and greeted her.

'Is that Maureen? Are you inside?' he asked, the urgency back in his voice, and it occurred to her he had been keeping her on the phone to make sure she got indoors safely. The balloon of hope—and tenderness—pressed against her larynx, cutting off her air supply.

'Yes, I'm in the kitchen with Maureen,' she said, taking off her coat one-handed while still clinging to her phone with the other.

'I have to go,' he said. 'I've got a meeting. I'll send the car at seven—make sure you're in it,' he added. 'And no more unaccompanied walks, understand?'

'Nico's barely in bed by seven,' she countered. 'Seven-thirty would be better.'

'Seven-fifteen, and no stalling—or I'm coming over there *now* to get you.'

'You can't—you've got a meeting.'

'Bronte, I own the company,' he said, the warning in his voice unequivocal.

'Okay! Sheesh, don't get your panties in a twist,' she said, trying to inject the lightness back into the conversation that had been comprehensively lost—and get the desperate excitement of being wanted, being cherished, out of her system.

'Fine,' he murmured, the rough laugh echoing in her heart. 'I'll see you at the penthouse at seven-thirty,' he said. 'Prepare for your panties to be history by seven thirty-one.'

Bronte stared at the phone after he had ended the call, her heart jolting in her chest like a jackhammer.

'Is everything okay, dear?' Maureen asked as she hung up Bronte's coat.

Bronte shoved the phone into the back pocket of her jeans. 'Yes,' she said.

But her galloping pulse and her trembling fingers told a different story.

* * *

'Mr Blackstone,' Lisa greeted Lukas as he stepped out of the penthouse elevator. 'Is everything all right?'

'Of course,' he said, unable to hide his smile as he tucked his phone into his jacket pocket. Only four hours until he would see Bronte again. Yesterday had been torture. Even though he had come to enjoy the trips he made to see the boy—Nico was a smart, funny and fascinating kid who had somehow wormed his way into Lukas's affections—being with Bronte and not being able to touch her was a special form of torture.

Take that moment at the end of his visit to Regent's Park yesterday, when he'd been bidding Nico and Bronte goodbye. Stifling the urge to sweep her into his arms and carry her off to the nearest bedroom had nearly killed him.

Tonight he was fixing at least some of his frustration. Tonight she was staying with him the entire night, and he was not going to countenance any more arguments on the subject. If it came to it, he actually was prepared to tie her to the bed.

He understood her devotion to Nico. He was pretty damn devoted to the kid too now. But no harm would be done by having the boy taken to Nursery by Maureen a few mornings a week.

He hated watching her drag herself out of their bed in the middle of the night after he'd exhausted her. The last time she'd been to see him, he'd actually regretted the sex he'd initiated in the shower. What with keeping their liaison a secret from everyone but his most trusted employees and the need to limit his access to her, he was making enough compromises already. It was starting to fuel a need to see her, to be with her, that didn't feel all that healthy.

When was the last time he'd rung up a woman in the middle of the day and harassed her to come over to his place? Or contemplated dropping an important finance meeting to see her? But he knew if she'd given him the go-ahead he would have been in his car within ten seconds flat.

'Are you sure you're all right, sir?' Lisa asked as they headed down the corridor towards the meeting room.

'Yes, why do you ask?' he said, noticing her astonished expression for the first time.

'You just took the elevator down to the office instead of the emergency stairs.'

He frowned, the observation giving him pause. 'I didn't have time to take the stairs,' he said, but couldn't help the prickle of unease at Lisa's revelation.

He always avoided elevators. Just like he had always insisted on having his living spaces open-plan and full of as much natural light as was humanly possible.

He hated to be crowded or to feel confined. The mechanical hiss of elevator doors closing had always unnerved him. But as he'd been absorbed in his call with Bronte, he'd walked into the metal box without even thinking about what he was doing.

And the usual cold sweat, the usual grinding fear hadn't materialised, because he'd been way too distracted by the sound of her voice, and the thought of her wandering the streets without the necessary protection.

'Have you got the report from Clinton on the final figures for the Maldives launch?' he asked, cutting off Lisa's line of questioning. Just because he'd been able to ride in an elevator for the first time in… Well, for ever. It did not have to be significant.

'Yes, Mr Blackstone.' Lisa handed the report over, looking almost as flustered as he felt.

He flicked through the pages until he got to the final profit and loss calculation, but as he stared at the figures he couldn't seem to remember the projected calculations he would usually have on instant recall to compare with the final ones.

The pulse of heat, which hadn't quite subsided since he'd threatened to tie Bronte to the bed, echoed in his groin.

Forcing himself to focus—on something other than Bronte—he walked into the meeting room ahead of Lisa and dumped the printout on the large walnut wood table. The executives he'd insisted travel to London from his landmark hotels in New York, Paris, Sydney and Hong Kong all jumped.

'Welcome, ladies and gentlemen. Thanks for making the trip,' he said and then stalled—as a vision of Bronte, laughing in the garden yesterday afternoon as he attempted to pitch the ball to Nico, blasted into his brain like a shaft of pure sunshine. He could still recall her unruly hair, that beautiful mix of auburn and russet and strawberry blonde, sticking out from under the ball cap he'd bought for her. Her smoky chuckle had rippled across his skin and made his heart thunder against his ribs.

His chest tightened and he lost his train of thought as his executives all stared back at him with a mixture of concern and expectation on their faces.

Dammit, Blackstone. Stop thinking about her.

But he couldn't focus; he couldn't even seem to remember what the heck these people were here to do. All he could focus on was Bronte and how much he'd wanted to hold her in that moment, to gather her up in his arms and kiss her senseless. And despite the surge of arousal that accompanied the thought, the desire, the need felt like more than that—wrapping around his heart like a warm blanket and smothering the monsters which had lurked for so long in dark corners.

Lisa's phone blared out a ringtone, shattering the silence.

She answered it and her eyes widened. 'Okay, I'll let him know.'

She cupped her hand over the receiver and said under her breath, so that only he could hear, 'It's Dex. He says it's about Bronte.'

He didn't wait to hear more, but grabbed the phone and marched out of the room. 'Make my excuses,' he said over his shoulder and headed into a private office next door.

'Dex, what's going on with Bronte?' Was she sick? Had something happened to her? The thundering in his chest became painful and he began to feel light-headed as the blood raced out of his head and flooded into his heart.

The flop sweat was back, dampening his shirt—the monstrous thoughts careering through his mind more terrifying than every one of his childhood nightmares. He wrenched open the button on his collar, loosened his tie, struggling to get enough air into his lungs to stay upright as his PR chief began to speak.

'I've just had a call from one of my contacts at Sleb Hunt,' Dex said, mentioning one of the most intrusive Internet gossip sites. 'They've got pictures of your nephew's aunt leaving an abortion clinic this morning.'

'What?' he croaked, his mind failing to compute the news.

'According to my sources, she's not having an abortion,' Dex continued as the decibel level in Lukas's ears rose to deafening and his thundering heart began to choke him. 'She was only there for pregnancy advice and she's been referred to a doctor for antenatal care. The even better news: the press are already speculating the kid is yours. Please tell me it is,' Dex added and for the first time Lukas caught the febrile excitement in the man's tone. 'Because this could be the major coup we've been waiting for with the family demographic on social media.'

But Lukas couldn't make any sense of the words any more. Because the only thing that kept going through his mind was the image of Bronte as she'd been yesterday— sweet, seductive, happy, the veneer of innocence and acceptance capturing his heart—and the shattering truth.

She's pregnant and she didn't tell me.

He wanted to be angry. But all he felt was betrayed. The frozen feeling numbed his brain, dragging him back to the lowest point in his life. Aged seven, the bandage on his face itching, his head aching with the effort to hold back the sobs locked in his throat, his limbs limp with exhaustion after the endless nightmares filled with monsters he knew were real.

Paying the ransom would have been a bad business move, Lukas.

'Lukas, are you still there?' Garvey's hectoring voice pulled him back.

'Sure,' he said, clearing his throat. His larynx felt as if someone had sandpapered it.

'So is the kid yours?' Garvey asked.

'Yeah, it's mine.' The surge of possessiveness was all-consuming—and finally forced the anger at her deception to the fore. To cover the hollow ache.

Garvey cursed. 'Why didn't you tell me sooner, buddy? We could have managed this situation a lot better. But hey, this is terrific news…' The PR chief's voice perked up considerably as he droned on about weddings and honeymoons and social media outreach, but Lukas had already tuned him out.

Bronte had lied to him, and carried on lying. Why was he even surprised? And why did it even matter?

Surely all that mattered now was the child. His child.

CHAPTER NINE

BRONTE STEPPED OUT of the limousine Lukas had sent to collect her, startled by the flash of lights.

'This way, Miss O'Hara.' James, her regular body-guard, ushered her towards the hotel's back entrance, shielding her from the muffled shouts.

She'd seen the paparazzi amassing outside the house before she'd left. It had to be a slow news day. But she didn't have the time or the emotional capacity to worry about them catching her coming into the Blackstone Park Lane.

She was already twenty minutes late because she'd decided to take a quick shower and dress up properly to see Lukas. She always came over in her jeans and T-shirts, because he never gave her enough time to change before sending the car. But this time she wanted to feel feminine and confident, ready to tell him news that she hoped would change his life, as well as hers, for the better.

She'd been expecting a call from Lukas during the ride over, demanding to know what was keeping her, but luckily it hadn't come. Because she wasn't sure she'd have been able to flirt with him again without blurting out the truth.

They headed down the corridor towards the hotel's opulent foyer, leaving the photographers behind them.

'What was that about?' she asked as they entered the penthouse elevator and James stabbed the button.

'I don't know, miss.'

She watched the floors whisk past on the digital panel, trying not to stress about the press. Once she began to show, questions would be asked about who her baby's father was—and hopefully she would be able to tell them, if everything went well tonight.

The elevator glided to a stop at the executive offices on the thirtieth floor and James stepped out.

'Aren't you coming up?' she asked. James always accompanied her to the penthouse, before disappearing discreetly.

He shook his head. 'Mr Blackstone told me to send you up alone.'

'Oh, okay,' she murmured as the doors closed, leaving her alone in the elevator.

The bubble of hope expanded like a balloon as the lift travelled up the final floor to Lukas's penthouse.

He was keen to see her. She pressed her hand to her abdomen, let her palm slide across the black silk of the short shift dress she had worn especially for him. The flutter of nerves and the tangle of anxiety were joined by the low hum of awareness and the bubble of hope that was now the size of a hot-air balloon.

Please let him be happy. Or at least not mad at the news.

The doors opened and her eyes tracked to the man she'd come to see standing on the opposite side of the room. He stood silhouetted against the night sky, his broad back stretching the seams of a tailored linen shirt as he stared out of the window. He looked as tall and indomitable as always but also strangely isolated and alone. The pang of compassion and empathy—and love—felt almost painful.

Hadn't they both been alone for too long? Protecting themselves from hurt. Surely this child could help bring them together instead of pulling them apart? Was it really too much to hope for?

'Lukas?' she said, hope thickening her voice.

He turned and she noticed he had a drink in his hand.

'You're late,' he said, the tone flat.

'I wanted to have a shower and change into something a bit more seductive.'

She stopped, feeling unsteady on the unaccustomed heels and stupidly shy as his gaze raked over her. Her pulse points jumped and jingled on cue.

'Nice,' he murmured, knocking back the liquor. He dropped the glass on a table. The loud crack made her jump.

Before she had a chance to catch her breath, he reached her. Plunging his fingers into her hair, he tilted her face up to his.

'You look good enough to eat, Bronte. As always,' he said, but there was something in his voice that felt sharp and brittle.

'Lukas, I need to speak to you,' she said, breathing heavily, the weight of arousal in her stomach joined by the renewed shimmer of anxiety. She could taste the liquor on his breath and see the glitter of temper in his eyes.

Was he angry with her for being twenty minutes late?

'Let's talk later,' he said, pressing her back until she bumped against the wall of the apartment. 'And screw first.'

The crudity shocked her, but not as much as the tidal wave of longing that slammed into her as his hand rode up her thigh under the short dress. His thumb settled on her clitoris, rubbing the swollen spot through the dampening gusset of her panties.

She jerked at the intimate touch, the devastatingly sure stroke.

'Lukas?' she said, desperately trying to grasp hold of what was wrong through the daze of passion. This didn't feel right. Didn't feel like the man she had teased and joked with earlier in the day. The man she had finally admitted to herself moments ago she was falling hopelessly in love with.

His lips fastened on her neck, sending shivering sensation down to her core as he continued to caress and cajole the slick folds through the lace. The confusion and anxiety dissipated, driven into submission by desperate yearning. Her head fell back, giving him better access as her body arched into his caresses, begging for his touch.

The sound of ripping fabric jolted her brain out of the erotic fog. But then he hooked one of her legs over his hip, spreading her wide and bringing her swollen clitoris into intimate contact with the thick ridge in his pants.

'Wait, Lukas... I...' she managed, making one last desperate effort to focus her thoughts on something other than the driving needs of her body. She needed to slow him down. To tell him about the pregnancy before they made love again.

'You're soaking wet for me, baby,' he said, the casual endearment one he'd never used before. Why did it sound vaguely insulting?

His face came up from her neck and his knuckles brushed against the hot flesh of her sex as he released his erection. 'Do you really want me to wait? Tell me the truth?'

The hunger in his voice was tempered by something

else, something both terrifying and exulting. And guilt burned under the pulsing need. 'No,' she said.

She hadn't been honest with him. Perhaps now was the time to start.

'I didn't think so,' he said.

Grasping both her thighs, he hoisted her up and impaled her on his straining erection in one solid thrust. She sobbed, the brutal pleasure shocking in its intensity as she stretched to receive him.

He moved, thrusting deep, forcing her to take all of him. She groaned, clinging on to his shoulders, the pleasure raw and rough and unstoppable.

Capturing one straining nipple with his mouth, he suckled hard through lace and silk. Arrows of sensation joined the ruthless conflagration and combined with the wellspring of emotion she no longer had any control over, bombarding her, battering her. She cried out as she crashed over, her body disintegrating into a million tiny, insignificant pieces, her will no longer her own.

It felt like an eternity but could only have been a few moments before Lukas could force his fingers to release their grip on Bronte's thighs.

You weren't going to touch her.

Recriminations seared his brain as he lifted her off him. She flinched and an agonising feeling of regret flooded through him.

Shut it down. Ignore it. She lied to you. She doesn't give a damn about you.

He waited for her to find her feet before letting go of her arm to zip his fly. Seeing the tattered remains of her panties, he bent to pick them up. And handed them to her.

He shouldn't have touched her, but now he had it only made him more determined to set the plan he'd been working on during the afternoon into motion. The physical chemistry between them hadn't dimmed. Maybe he'd been sidetracked, tricked by his own libido into thinking for a few dumb moments that what they had could be more. That he wanted it to be more. But it didn't need to be more.

'Lukas?' she asked, searching his face as she stuffed the ragged lace into her purse with trembling fingers. 'Is something wrong?'

'You could say that,' he snapped, leading with anger. He had a right to be furious, dammit. 'When were you planning to tell me about the pregnancy?'

A guilty flush rose to her hairline. But the flags of colour blazing on her cheeks and the shocked confusion shadowing her eyes only made her look more beautiful.

'How do you know?' she managed at last.

'You were spotted leaving an abortion clinic this morning—by a photographer.' He glanced at his watch. 'The shots hit the Internet about an hour ago.' He wondered why she didn't know about it already—Garvey had called twice, desperate to get him to issue some sort of official statement.

'I see,' she said, guilt lighting up her face now. 'I'm sorry. I should have told you sooner,' she said.

No kidding.

'I should tell you now—I'm not going to have an abortion,' she added, her voice clear and determined. The confirmation had a strange effect on the hollow ache in his stomach.

He'd never wanted to be a father. Had always known it wasn't something he was cut out for. And he'd already started to figure out ways to manage his involvement with this child. But, even so, the pregnancy didn't terrify him the way he might have expected. No. That would be her, and the way she made him feel. And the fear that he might already be in too deep to pull out.

'I know you're not,' he said. 'Which is why we're getting married. As soon as possible.'

He'd put the wheels in motion this afternoon, and had been ready to present her with the deal as soon as she'd arrived. They'd gotten distracted, sure. But making her his wife instead of his mistress was necessary now. She'd chosen to have the child. But it was his child too, and he was never going to be left out of the decision-making again.

He planned to support it and give it his name—and his protection.

He didn't let people get too close. But somehow she'd gotten close enough to him in the last six weeks to make him forget that if you did people hurt you, they betrayed you. So from now on their relationship was going to be on his terms, not hers.

'What…?' She looked stunned by the offer. He supposed he should be glad she hadn't planned this pregnancy to trick him into marriage—just one of the reasons for her subterfuge that he'd considered in the last four hours. But he didn't feel glad; he just felt numb.

'You heard me,' he said. 'I'll need you to sign a prenup. But I think you'll be impressed with the generosity of the contract.'

'The contract,' she said, looking appalled as well as stunned. 'That sounds more like a business arrangement than a marriage.'

'Because that's exactly what it will be.'

'I can't accept that,' she said. 'I don't want to marry you under those circumstances.' She covered her stomach with one hand, as if trying to shield him from the life inside her. The gesture had anger pulsing in his forehead.

He might not be cut out to be a father, but did she think so little of him that she thought he would hurt their child?

'It's not a request,' he said. 'I'm not asking you to marry me, I'm telling you.'

'I don't get a choice?' she murmured, looking distressed now.

To hell with that. He wasn't the one who had decided to keep this child a secret.

'You had your choice when you decided to tell me you were taking contraception when you weren't. When you decided not to tell me you were pregnant. And when you visited an abortion clinic and got photographed by the paparazzi.'

Moisture filled her eyes, which she blinked away furiously. 'But I'm not going to have a termination. Is that why you're so angry?'

He let his gaze roam down to her abdomen, confused again by the strange stirring in his chest at the thought of this child. Their child. Living inside her. Strictly speaking, he should be furious about that because he'd always been so careful never to get into this predicament. But the thought of the child, the reality of the child wasn't the problem—it was the roller coaster of emotions that had been overwhelming him ever since he'd discovered its existence. Hell, before then—ever since he'd let himself fall into an affair he didn't seem to have any control over.

'We both got you pregnant,' he said. 'And what you decide to do with your own body is your choice,' he said. 'So no, that's not why I'm angry.'

The look of relief on her face only spiked more of those tumultuous emotions that he didn't understand and didn't want to understand. He just wanted them to go away.

'Then what is it? If you think you have to marry me

because of this, you don't. I made a choice to have this baby and I would never force you to be involved.'

'I'm already involved,' he said. 'No child of mine is going to grow up without the Blackstone name. Which means you're going to have to have it too.'

'You can give the baby your name without us being married.'

'That's not going to work for me,' he said because she obviously didn't get it. That this was about control. About the fact he couldn't live without her yet. And he didn't want her to live without him. Until he'd gotten this compulsion out of his system they would be stuck together. So they might as well be stuck together in matrimony. It would give him rights, not just over his child but over her.

Pulling his phone out of his pocket as she continued to stare at him, the distress in her eyes palpable now, he keyed in Lisa's number. 'Lisa, you can send the legal team in now.'

Bronte would get a generous monthly allowance for the rest of her life. And his child would be sent to the best schools, the best colleges. It would never want for anything.

'You can't force me to marry you, Lukas.' She was shaking now, her voice trembling. He didn't care. He wasn't going to let himself care.

'Yes, I can,' he said, finally allowing a little of his fury with her—with the whole situation—to show. 'I'm a very rich man, Bronte. You're already living in a house I bought you. You kept my nephew's existence from me for three years and you tried to do the same with my own child. How do you think a judge is going to view that when I sue for custody of both of them?' It was a threat he'd made unintentionally before, but he was playing hard ball now. The means always justified the ends. He'd lost sight of that in the last six weeks—but it was something his father had taught him when he was seven. If you let your emotions get in the way of what you wanted to achieve, you'd never achieve anything.

Her face blanched, the last of the colour leaching out of her cheeks.

'I still think I'd win,' she said, but her bottom lip was trembling. 'I'm Nico's legal guardian; you've only known him for a few months.'

'Because you kept his existence from me,' he countered.

'At his mother's request. It's still…'

'You really want to take me on, Bronte? To put Nico through a long protracted custody battle after what he's already been through?' It was a low blow. He didn't want to hurt the boy, but he was through playing things her way.

'Why are you even doing this? You can see both the baby and Nico as much as you want. I would never limit your custody. Why do you have to marry me?'

Why? No way would he tell her the whole truth. Because it would make him feel weak and needy. And it would expose him in a way he'd never allowed himself to be exposed. Not since he was seven years old and he'd found himself locked in the dark with no way out. So he seized on the reasoning Garvey had spouted at him four hours ago, when this nightmare had begun.

'The company has spent the last five years developing and investing in the Blackstone's Deluxe Family Resort brand. Our first property opens in two weeks' time. And you've just blown the whole press and PR strategy out of the water. Social media is already awash with speculation that the baby you were attempting to abort is mine. I'm the villain in that scenario, not you.'

'But I wasn't even considering a termination. The clinic you're talking about is a pregnancy advisory service too. I was never going to have a termination.'

'So I get cast as a deadbeat dad instead? A guy who gets someone pregnant and then walks away,' he said. 'Our research shows that it's women, mothers, who generally make the decision on family vacation destinations.'

'You're forcing me to marry you so you can sell vacations?' she said, the agonised distress turning to incredulity.

'What we're talking about is a five-billion-dollar investment—which will be dead in the water, according to my PR guy, if we don't get married.' It wasn't, strictly speaking, the truth. Garvey had simply said a marriage would be a great PR story to support the launch. And right at this very second, he didn't give a damn about the money, the investment or even the branding that they'd been working on for five years. All he cared about was sealing up the black hole in the pit of his stomach and shoving all those emotions he hadn't felt in years back in the box marked 'don't give a damn'.

'The Maldives development is part of an eco-friendly project which supplies a sustainable living for over twenty thousand local people in one capacity or another. That project goes bust and all those people are out of a job. You really want to be responsible for that?'

He could see he'd got to her when her eyes flickered away from his, the colour still riding high on her cheeks. Eventually she shook her head. 'What do you want me to do?'

'We issue a press release tonight and then head for the new resort tomorrow to get married. We can stay there for a week's honeymoon before it opens.' Given what had just happened against the wall of his apartment, he figured they'd find ways to pass the time that didn't involve him making any more emotional commitments he wasn't comfortable with.

'But I can't just leave Nico for a week,' she said, her voice breaking on the words.

'Nico will be fine with Maureen. You can contact him by Skype every day. We can even fly Nico and Maureen out for the launch at the end of the honeymoon.'

'No, I don't want him to be part of this PR stunt,' she said, her voice firm, giving him a glimpse of the tigress he'd first met the night she'd confronted him at Blackstone's Full Moon Ball.

The surge of desire was swift. But the surge of admiration was more disconcerting. Even if he would never be able to trust her any more than he'd ever been able to trust anyone, at least he knew she would make a good mother to his child. The way she'd already made a good mother, in all but name, to his brother's son.

'Nico doesn't have to come,' he conceded, forcing himself to hide his disappointment. The boy would have gotten a major kick out of some of the kids' facilities at the resort, and he would have gotten a kick out of showing them to him. But she was right—they didn't need to involve the boy in this subterfuge. 'Garvey can put a spin on it either way,' he added.

'Can I ask you something?' She hesitated after he nodded. 'What happens after we get back from our fake honeymoon?'

The honeymoon wasn't going to be fake. Not in any of the ways that mattered. He sure as heck wasn't giving her a chance to back out of this marriage on a technicality because they hadn't consummated it. But he didn't figure there was much mileage in pointing that out now. Once they got to Blackstone Island, she'd be looking for a distraction as much as he was. Especially as the only people there were going to be the two of them and the staff.

'Afterwards, I guess I'll have to move into the place in Regent's Park for a while.'

'For how long?' she said dully.

'As long as it takes to convince people this marriage is real,' he said curtly.

And I get over the dumb urge to have you in my bed—and watch over you, and Nico and our baby, every damn minute of every day.

'Us playing happy families is going to be confusing for Nico,' she said flatly, her expression blanker than he'd ever seen it.

'Uh-huh, well, you should have thought about that before you lied to me about being on the Pill,' he said. The thought of having to live in that house knowing he could never be a part of that happy family was a new form of torture he hadn't even considered. She didn't care about him, had never cared about him. It seemed so obvious now.

She stiffened and looked out of the window at the gathering night. Then she wrapped her arms around her midriff in a defensive gesture that had shame snapping at his heels.

He pushed it away as the hollow pain in his stomach twisted.

She should have told him about the pregnancy a lot sooner. What right did she have to look so fragile, so overwhelmed?

Cupping her elbow, he tugged her round to face him. 'We'll figure out a way to make sure it doesn't confuse Nico. I do a lot of travelling, so I won't be around much anyway.' He allowed himself the luxury of glancing down at her belly. 'Once the baby's born, Nico will be far too busy welcoming his new cousin into the world to care about what's going on with us.'

'I suppose.' She chewed her bottom lip—the shot of desire was swift and unequivocal. 'But will you promise me one thing?'

He nodded, the tightening in his chest almost unbearable now. Why was this so hard? He was just doing what needed to be done. To protect his child.

'Don't let Nico know how much you dislike me.'

He frowned. 'That won't be a problem,' he said because he didn't dislike her, couldn't make himself dislike her… Even if he should.

CHAPTER TEN

'I WILL,' BRONTE MURMURED, her whole body trembling as she stood on the white sand beach and shielded her eyes against the mid-afternoon sun.

The minister continued to talk, but the words seemed to float above her head and drift out over a sea so blue it hurt her eyes.

She jolted as Lukas gripped her fingers. His hold was sure and firm as he slipped the wedding band onto her ring finger. The expensive white-gold reflected the sun's rays, mocking her, as a photographer appeared to take their picture.

The palm fronds fluttered in the warm sea breeze. And the feeling of unreality—of being in a deluxe but devastating dream—settled into her soul.

Lukas's palm pressed into the small of her back as he led her towards the entourage of staff and hotel executives who rushed forward to congratulate them.

'How are you holding up?' he murmured in her ear, his hand sliding down to her hip as he led her across the sand.

'Good, a little tired,' she replied. He'd been unbearably solicitous ever since she'd agreed to this sham marriage two days ago—which only made the situation more agonising.

If only she could hate him for forcing her into this.

But how could she? When she was already hopelessly in love with him.

She strained to keep a polite smile on her face during the hour that followed, as they sat down to an elaborate wedding feast. She barely swallowed a bite of the lavish array of dishes brought out with pomp and circumstance by the resort's chef and his staff.

She would have to spend the next week pretending to be a happy bride for the cameras—and goodness knew how much longer pretending to be making a happy family with Lukas when they returned to London—while secretly wishing all the time for the impossible—that their marriage didn't have to be a pretence. She was right back where she'd been as a little girl, standing on her father's doorstep, hoping for a love she wasn't going to get.

Finally the wedding meal was over and Lukas led her to a line of golf carts. She climbed into the lead vehicle with him. He drove past the hotel complex where she'd stayed the night before, alone in a luxury suite, after they'd arrived on the private island atoll in his jet.

'Where are we going?' she asked.

He glanced her way. 'To our honeymoon villa—it's on the other side of the island.'

But this isn't a real honeymoon.

Pain pierced Bronte's chest, slicing through the numbness that had enveloped her for the last forty-eight hours.

They arrived at the idyllic beachside villa. With a lap pool at the back and a large deck in front, the lavish three-room cottage looked like a romantic idyll.

The crystalline blue of the sea sparkled against the red and golds of the sun bleeding into the horizon as it began to set.

Bronte stood on the deck as a small troop of bell boys arrived to deliver their luggage. Her cases were packed full of the wardrobe of new clothes Lukas had employed a stylist to provide as a series of magazine photoshoots had been arranged over the next few days by his press chief Dex Garvey.

Just the thought of that exhausted her. But as she stood watching the sun sink into the sea, the thought of posing for the camera as Lukas's fake bride didn't feel anywhere near as overwhelming as actually having to spend six nights alone with him here.

Way to go, Bronte. Surely only you could manage to find yourself in one of the most beautiful and luxurious places on earth, living with a devastatingly attractive man who you're already in love with and still be miserable.

The thought of their time alone together had terrified her over the last two days—while she'd prepared herself and Nico for her departure.

'Will he be my daddy now?'

Nico's wide-eyed question yesterday morning, just before Lukas's car had arrived to take her to the airport, still haunted her.

She tuned out the sound of Lukas on his mobile phone, talking to one of his executives in the beach cottage's lavish living area.

The quiet lap of the water against the deck brought with it the salty scent of the sea and the fragrant island flowers. But as she absorbed the beauty of their surroundings her hand strayed to her belly. She pressed her palm to the flat curve of her stomach and imagined herself in seven months' time.

Her chest expanded. They were going to have a child together. A child that deserved to be loved and cherished by both its parents, the way she had never been.

Maybe Lukas couldn't love her, but what about their child?

She'd been blindsided by his brutal decision to black-mail her into this marriage of convenience. She had been reeling ever since that devastating showdown in his of-fice. She'd collapsed in on herself—all her confidence and hope had drained away and she'd become the same pathetic shadow of herself she'd been once before—when her father had rejected her.

But they were married now, for better or for worse. She'd agreed to do this thing, but why did she have to abide by Lukas's rules? If she didn't have the confidence, the energy to fight for herself, couldn't she at least find the confidence to fight for their child?

She heard Lukas approach behind her. Her heartbeat pummelled her eardrums as his arm banded around her waist and he drew her back against him. His lips ca-ressed her neck in the spot he knew would drive her wild. Shivers of awareness she couldn't disguise bom-barded her body.

'How about we go straight to bed?' he murmured. 'This damn marriage ought to have some advantages.'

She turned and butted her forearms against his chest. She wanted him—it was pointless trying to deny it. But there was more at stake here than just sex.

'So what's the plan here? We sleep together, pretend to be married and then what?' she said, her temper finally helping to snap her out of the fog that had descended when he'd insisted on this marriage.

'We're not pretending,' he said. 'This is a real mar-riage—it says so on the paperwork you signed.'

She tugged out of his arms. 'That would be the paper-work that has a sell-by date on it, would it?'

His frown deepened.

'When exactly is that sell-by date, Lukas?' she con-tinued, her heart hurting at the blank look on his face.

'When the baby's born? Once the press are convinced you're not a deadbeat dad? When you're bored with sleeping with me? Because I'm assuming you get to make that choice, not me.' Why was she letting him turn their marriage into something cold and sterile and businesslike when it could be so much more than that?

'Hey, calm down.' He grasped her elbow, tugged her back to him. Then cupped her cheek in his palm. 'You're tired. It's been a long couple of days, I get that. We don't have to sleep together tonight. It can wait,' he said, completely missing the point.

His lips tipped up in a tight smile, but still she could see the strain around his mouth.

'But we are going to consummate it, Bronte,' he said. 'I'm not having you slip out of this deal on a technicality.'

She stared at him and suddenly something dawned on her that she hadn't let herself hope for. What if this marriage meant more to him too?

Why had she accepted all his cold, calculating reasons for demanding this marriage? Was it because a part of that scared, rejected little girl still lurked inside her?

'Sex isn't going to solve this problem, Lukas.' She shrugged away from his touch as she gathered all her courage and forced herself to face all the fears and insecurities that had lived inside her for so long, and held her back without her even knowing it. 'Do you want to know why I agreed to this marriage?'

He stared at her, the look in those onyx eyes both wary and tense. 'You agreed because I threatened to take Nico away from you,' he said, but his gaze flicked away from her—and she finally acknowledged what she had known all along in her subconscious when he'd made the threat… He would never have followed through on it.

His gaze dipped to her belly. 'And because you're having my child.'

'I guess I wanted to convince myself those were the reasons. But it's actually much simpler than that. I agreed to marry you, Lukas, because I love you.'

'What?' The flash of fear in his eyes was all the answer she needed to all the questions she'd been asking ever since they had met. 'Damn it, Bronte, don't say that.'

'Why not?' she said as she finally admitted the whole truth to herself.

She'd been scared too, scared of admitting how she really felt about him—not just to him but to herself. Because of her father's rejection all those years ago. And she'd been scared of telling him about the baby. Because she was terrified of his response.

And why was she so scared? Because she'd convinced herself, deep down, that she didn't deserve love or respect. She didn't deserve to be cherished. That she was better off alone. That she could fill her life with loving Nico—and loving this baby—and that would be enough.

But that was crap. Because the truth was she wanted so much more than that. She deserved more than that. They both did. And so did their child. But if she wanted more, she was going to have to fight for it.

If she allowed this marriage to start based on a lie, if she allowed Lukas to hide his feelings the way she had tried to hide hers, the chance of building something lasting, something strong and real and worthwhile would die before it could ever be born.

'You mustn't fall in love with me,' he said and she could hear the fear plainly in his voice now. She wondered if he could hear it too. 'You'll only regret it when this marriage has to end.'

'Why does it have to end?' She finally asked the question that had been lurking inside her for two days. The question she'd been too cowardly to voice.

'Don't make me say it.'

'You owe me an answer,' she said.

'Fine.' He sighed, the sound so resigned it broke her heart. 'It will end eventually…when you realise I can't love you back.'

'Why can't you?'

Lukas's guts felt as if they were being torn out. How had it come to this? How could he have not seen this coming? He was supposed to be the one in control and yet Bronte had blindsided him again.

Not with that sweet, sexy, responsive body this time, but with her far too open and generous heart.

She didn't know what the hell she was saying. He hadn't meant to hurt her like this. His anger at her deception over the pregnancy had died as soon as she had agreed to this devil's bargain. And in the last few days he'd acknowledged the real reasons he'd blackmailed her into this… He wanted her even though he knew he could never deserve her. Or make her happy.

And now she would discover the truth. Because he would have to come clean with her. To tell her why he was damaged goods. Why, despite all the trappings of wealth and success he'd clung to for so long, he had been emotionally bankrupt—a broken human being—ever since he was seven years old. It was why he had never been able to properly grieve for his own brother, why he had found it so hard to bond with Nico, why he'd tried so hard to control any feelings he had for Bronte and the boy. Why he knew that, despite what she said, all he could ever really offer their child was financial security. And why this marriage could never be real, why it would never last.

'What happened, Lukas? Was it what they did to you when you were kidnapped?' She lifted her hand and touched her fingertips to the scar on his cheek. She stroked the ruined skin, the shimmer of tears in her eyes only destroying him more. 'Is that why you're so terrified of letting me in? You're still traumatised by those events?'

He grasped her finger, dragged it away from his face and shook his head.

He owed her this much. She deserved to know how broken he was. So she could protect herself.

He stared out at the ocean, the ghostly shadows as the moon rose over the horizon shimmering over the sea. The luxury surroundings here were in sharp contrast to the dingy, dirty room where they'd once kept him—but he felt just as trapped, just as helpless.

His stomach tightened into hard knots, sweat dampening the linen of his shirt as pain seared his skin. But it wasn't that memory that had haunted him in nightmares for years afterwards. And made him feel so worthless.

'I used to wet the bed after it happened, after I was home again,' he said, his voice rough to his own ears. 'I had nightmares, of course. I still struggle with elevators. I'm not great in confined spaces,' he added, realising she was the first person he'd ever been able to admit that to. 'They kept me in a root cellar. I was terrified—of course I was. But the truth is, apart from the one time they cut me, to persuade my father to pay up, they mostly ignored me.'

'Did you get counselling?' she asked, with the fierce compassion in her tone that he had somehow come to adore, to rely on, without even realising it. 'To handle the trauma?'

He huffed out a laugh, the sound as raw and hopeless as he felt. 'Not precisely. My father—who was generally a distant figure in my life—sent for me one day to go to his offices in Manhattan. It had been over a month since the kidnapping and he was annoyed that I was still wetting the bed. And that my school reports hadn't improved. He told me, in no uncertain terms, to snap out of it. That I was his heir. And not just because I was the older of the two of us, but also because he believed I had the better temperament. Alexei was like our mother, he said. Wild and flighty and easily diverted. A hedonist who didn't know the meaning of responsibility or restraint.'

'But the two of you were only seven years old!' she said, aghast.

He shoved his fists into the pockets of his pants, the evening breeze cooling the clammy sweat on his skin.

'You know what's weird? I never questioned that assessment. It never even occurred to me that maybe Alexei's subsequent behaviour—the drinking, the drugs, the women, the reckless pursuit of pleasure at all costs—was as much of a plea for our father's affection as my own behaviour. I always bought into the lie that it was because Alexei was infertile—or thought he was—that he never believed he had anything to live for. But the truth is, Alexei knew long before that, just like I did, that our father didn't give a damn about either of us.'

'What happened when you went to see him, Lukas?' she asked.

'He told me he'd chosen not to pay the ransom. The Feds had requested he make it available, to facilitate the sting operation they had in mind the day after they'd cut my face. But he refused. He boasted about it to me.'

'What?' The horror etched on her face tore at that place deep inside he'd kept hidden, protected, buried for so long. Ever since his father had sat him down in his office and told him he wasn't as important as Blackstone's business reputation.

'It wasn't the money, he told me, it was the principle of the thing.'

'That scumbag.' Bronte's fury seemed to pierce the numb feeling that had permeated his life for so long.

But he resisted it. He didn't want to feel. Didn't want to open himself to that kind of hurt again.

'The truth is I've spent my whole life trying to be the same cold, ruthless bastard he was. And I've succeeded.'

Grasping his face, she dragged his gaze to hers. He stiffened, startled to see a tear roll down her cheek. Her face flushed with anger.

'That's nonsense, Lukas. You're not cold or ruthless. And, just for the record, you were worth every single penny of that bloody ransom.'

He clasped her hands, hopelessly torn by the urge to pull away from that fierce love and the desire to sink into it at the same time.

'You have to understand, Bronte, I can't love you,' he said, the words coming out on a husky breath, because now she knew exactly how broken he was. 'Because I'm simply not capable of that depth of emotion. Not any more.'

Oh, Lukas. You idiot.

Tears welled in Bronte's eyes but she blinked them back. She mustn't fall apart now, or she'd never be able to say to him everything that needed to be said.

'I don't know what you think love is, Lukas. But it isn't some grand romantic gesture; it's all the little things you do to show people you care about them, that they matter to you.'

'Are you trying to tell me you're happy to love me, knowing I can never love you back?' he said, sounding frustrated now and so confused. 'Because that's nuts.'

'No,' she replied. 'That's not what I'm saying.'

'Then what *are* you saying?' he said, his voice rising with frustration. But she could hear the anguish beneath, and the insecurity. And it was all the opening she needed.

'Can I tell you about something that happened to me, when I was a little girl?'

He sent her a stiff nod.

'When I was a baby my father walked out on me and Darcy and my mum. Like your father, he was selfish and shallow and he only ever thought about himself. I was so young when it happened I didn't even remember him, but I'd built up a picture in my head of this ideal guy. Then one day my mum told us we were going to meet him. I was so excited. But when he opened the door that day he didn't even make eye contact with Darcy and me. He told my mother he'd "moved on", he told us to go away, and so we did. And that was the last time I saw him.'

'That bastard.'

She forced a breath past constricted lungs, the fury in Lukas's expression all the courage she needed to continue. 'I was devastated, but I buried that hurt and that unhappiness. I told myself not to care, not to love, not to want that kind of commitment from anyone, to protect myself from ever feeling that devastated, that rejected again.'

How foolish not to realise much sooner that Lukas had been doing exactly the same thing with her and Nico.

'But can't you see,' Lukas said, 'I'm damaged the same way he was, the way my father was. You need to protect yourself from me. Loving me will only lead to more of...'

'Shh.' She touched his cheek to silence him. The scar tensed, but the devastation, the guilt in his eyes was like a benediction.

'What I wanted to say, to explain, was that I've realised something very important in the last few weeks and months knowing you, seeing you with Nico and being with you.' She blushed. 'Both in bed and out of it. Something I didn't realise fully until I said those vows on the beach today and I wanted so much for them to be real.'

He sighed, shook his head. 'They can't ever be real. I…'

'Lukas…' She touched her fingertip to his lips. 'I'm not finished.' She smiled at his frown—the evidence that he was very rarely interrupted somehow endearing. 'What I wanted to say was that for months after that day I relived that moment on my father's doorstep hundreds of times in my head. I would imagine that he looked at me and Darcy and he told us he loved us and he always would. Eventually I had to kill that dream because it was only making me more unhappy, more insecure. But you know what I've realised since meeting you?'

Lukas shook his head, his frown deepening.

'I've realised that it wouldn't have made a difference what he did or said that day. Because during all the years of my childhood, before that day and after that day, he'd never once *shown* me he loved me. He wasn't there for birthdays and Christmases… He wasn't there for my first day of school or my last. He wasn't there for all the times when I was scared or lonely or needed comfort and reassurance. For all the times I needed to know I was cherished and important. He wasn't there, because he'd chosen not to be. But ever since I met you, Lukas, you *have* been there. You've shown me, and Nico, in so many little ways, and some pretty enormous ones—bone marrow donations and twenty-eight-point-five-million-pound palaces most definitely included—that you *do* care, that we matter. And that's what love is.'

'The bone marrow was a trick of genetics,' he said, still frowning. 'And the house was just money.'

'Well, thank goodness for that trick of genetics,' she said, knowing it had been much more than that. 'And it's not the amount the house cost that's important,' she said. Even though in some ways it was, because he'd bought that place for two people he didn't even know, whereas his own father had refused to pay twenty-eight-point-five times less than that to make his own son safe. 'What's important is why you bought it for us. You wanted us to be safe. To be secure. And that matters. Just like when you came round three days ago to show Nico how to play ball, or when you spent hours building a Lego house for an explorer you'd never heard of the first time you came to see him. You showed Nico he matters to you, even though you were scared of making that commitment. And every time you tried to seduce me into staying the night at your penthouse because you were worried I was too tired to go home, or rang me up in a panic because I had gone out without my bodyguards, you showed me that I mattered to you too.'

'I only did what any person would do; you're settling for too little, Bronte.'

'*Any* person?' she said, raising her eyebrows at him. 'Like your father? Like mine?'

'They were damaged people.'

'And you're not. That's the point.'

'Even if that were true,' he said, 'and that's a very big *if*, it still doesn't mean I can give you and Nico what you need. Emotionally speaking.'

Yes, it did, she thought. But she didn't have to convince him of that yet. He would discover it in time. All the goodness, the tenderness, the sensitivity inside him, the huge capacity for love he had denied existed for so long, would be self-evident to him too, eventually. All she had to do now was give them the chance to explore all those possibilities.

'You don't have to worry about giving us anything, Lukas.' Although the fact he did worry totally proved her point. 'All you need to worry about is whether you want this marriage to be *more* than a convenience. *More* than a contract between two business associates. *More* than a means of giving your child your name. And keeping all the very nice people here employed and this resort a success. Because if you do, I do too.'

'Yes, damn it.' The words shuddered out of Lukas on an anguished breath.

He grasped her waist, unable to hold himself back from touching her a moment longer. He pressed into her body, banded his hands around her slender waist as she lifted up on tiptoe and pressed her lips to his. He could taste the salt of her tears and feel the urgency of his own arousal. He let his hand drop, to grasp her hips and pull her against the straining heat of his erection.

'But what if this is all I can give you?' he said, the words wrenched from him. 'What if this is all I've got?'

'It's not,' she said with a certainty that humbled him, her face full of love and acceptance. And complete and utter faith.

It scared him to death.

He should draw back, should stop touching her. He couldn't have sex with her under these circumstances. But all those dark desires, all those driving needs—to be wanted, to be loved—broke over him and he found himself lifting her into his arms.

Just this once, let them do this thing with no subterfuge, no lies between them.

She wrapped her legs around his waist as he marched

into the bedroom. He dropped her on the bed, then tore off his clothes, and watched her scramble out of hers. He fell on her like a starving man, licking and nipping at her breasts, fuller now because of her pregnancy. He touched the swollen seam of flesh, felt her jolt in response as he tested her readiness.

'Take me, Lukas. I need you inside me now.'

Grasping at soft flesh, he plunged deep. She widened her hips, taking him deeper still as he ploughed into the welcoming heat. He tried to hold back—he wanted to make this good for her, as good as it was for him. But then she tightened around him like a vice, massaging his length as she climaxed, and an agonised shout was ripped from him as he crashed into orgasm.

He lifted off her with an effort, scared to crush her. Then held on to her, his heartbeat slowing, his limbs heavy with exhaustion as he listened to her breathing.

He lifted the sheet and draped it over her, the image of her heavy with their child in the months ahead making his hands tremble. He'd kidded himself that this marriage was to protect his business, to protect her, to protect their baby. But it had never been about that. It had always been about stealing the one thing he was terrified he needed beyond everything else. Her.

But now he was very much afraid he would never be able to let her go.

Her hand covered his and he was forced to look into her eyes. Those deep emerald pools that had always captivated him.

'I love you, Lukas. And I'm going to keep on loving you. And, for now, it doesn't matter if you think you can love me or not. Because I know you can.' Gripping his hand, she pressed it to her belly. 'We both do.'

His eyes felt gritty, the surface of them raw and painful with tears he hadn't allowed himself to shed since he'd sat in his father's office all those years ago.

'But why does it matter if I love you?' he murmured, knowing there was no *if* about it. 'If I still end up hurting you?' His gaze travelled down to her belly, where her hand covered his. 'Both of you? And Nico?'

Bronte's heart lifted and swelled at his gruff, agonised words. He looked lost and mildly terrified. And she knew precisely how he felt, because she had felt exactly the same way when she'd first become captivated by him—this dominant, frustrating, possessive, infuriatingly overprotective man. But she didn't feel that way any more. They had a long way to go before he would fully believe what a wonderful father and husband he would be. It would take them both some time to fully trust in this love, which was still so new and fresh and raw. But hope and honesty were powerful things. So much more powerful in the end than the rejections they had both suffered.

Lifting up, she straddled his hips, rejoicing in the dark intent in his gaze as those onyx eyes roamed over her and his hands clasped her waist.

Leaning forward, she let her hair drift over his cheek. The tips of her breasts grazed that solid, unyielding chest and she murmured, 'Is that your roundabout way of telling me you love me too?'

'I'm so busted,' he murmured.

She covered his hard lips, her heart lifting as she captured the stunned chuckle that finally signalled his surrender to hopes, to dreams… And, best of all, to love.

EPILOGUE

'Lukas, how's fatherhood? The new baby giving you and Bronte any sleep?'

'Bronte, are you enjoying your first family vacation since the birth? What's the Blackstone Island Resort like?'

'Nico, Nico, give us a wave.'

'The resort is wonderful,' Bronte shouted above the melee of shouted questions while Nico tugged her hand to lean past her and wave at the reporters, who were being held back by a phalanx of Blackstone security guards in Velana International Airport.

'Do not encourage them, you two,' her husband demanded as he wrapped his arm around her, shielding her and Nico from the burst of camera flashes.

'But I want them to know how great the resort is.' Bronte grinned at his grumpy expression as he ushered them into the private gangway.

'Publicising the resort is not your job,' he announced, as he led her and Nico towards the exit gate for their private flight to the Blackstone atoll, with their baby son cradled securely against his shoulder. 'That's Garvey's job and I intend to have words with him next time I see him,' he said, his expression thunderous. 'I very much doubt it's a coincidence that the press knew exactly when and where we would be changing planes.'

'Garvey's just doing his job,' Bronte said as they stepped aboard the private jet.

The staff greeted them then left them in the luxury cabin to prepare the plane for the final phase of their journey to the resort.

'Garvey is going to be looking for another job if he pulls any more stunts like this one. I've told him before—my family is off-limits,' he said, while absently patting their baby son's back to soothe the little boy, who had been woken up by all the commotion.

The picture he made, so competent, so caring, so devoted, and so different from the man she had met over a year ago, made Bronte's heart swell in her chest and her pulse batter her eardrums.

Their lives had been a whirlwind in the last ten months as they adjusted to marriage, to becoming a family, to welcoming Markus into their lives. But their love for each other had never faltered. And now Lukas believed in it too.

The honesty and the hope they had established on their wedding day, and the heat between them, had been a bedrock on which to build so much more. A foundation which had stayed strong while they met the many challenges of forming a new and exciting relationship, not just with each other but with Nico and little Markus too.

Bronte stroked his cheek, the scar rough against her palm, and smiled when his expression softened, the way it always did whenever he looked at her, or Nico, or Markus.

'Your transformation from playboy bachelor to devoted husband and father happens to be great press for the new brand. Deal with it.' She laughed at his exasperated expression as she repeated Dex Garvey's favourite phrase.

'Don't you start,' he muttered, rolling his eyes, but amusement quirked his lips and no small amount of pride flushed his cheeks.

'Daddy, Daddy, when are we going to get there?' Nico had let go of her hand as soon as they'd boarded and now raced up to Lukas to tug on his trouser leg.

Daddy.

Bronte's heartbeat stuttered, as it always did when she remembered the scene two months ago, after Nico had come back from his first day at pre-school in tears. Bronte had known something was terribly wrong, but the little boy had refused to talk about it until Lukas had returned from work.

'Why can't you be my daddy and Auntie Bronte be my mummy?' he had asked Lukas, his face heart-wrenchingly distraught. *'If baby Markus can have you as his mummy and daddy, why can't I? I don't want my mummy and daddy to be dead.'*

Lukas had looked at her over the little boy's head as he'd lifted Nico into his arms to try and soothe him, the agony she felt reflected in his eyes.

It wasn't something they'd ever discussed properly, other than to acknowledge that neither one of them wanted to usurp Alexei and Darcy's rightful place in Nico's life. But, as with so many things, Lukas had been the one to solve the problem. Simply and pragmatically, he'd negotiated with the little boy, man to man. He had sat Nico on his knee and explained to him that he was just as important to them as baby Markus and he always would be. But Nico had replied—being almost as tough a negotiator as Lukas—that his new friend Jake at school had told him being a nephew wasn't the same as being a son.

Lukas's gaze had connected with hers again and she had nodded, giving him her permission to find a solution. And, once again, her faith in his ability to handle Nico with tenderness and sensitivity and understanding had been rewarded.

He had told the little boy that while he would always have an extra mummy and daddy, who had loved him very much, of course Nico could call him and Bronte Mummy and Daddy too, if he wanted to, because that was exactly what they were to him.

Ever since, Nico had been calling them Mummy and Daddy as often as was humanly possible. And after ten hours on a plane with not nearly enough sleeping going on, his excitement at having his daddy's attention for two whole weeks had made his voice more than a little shrill.

'Will you take me on the water slides when we get there, Daddy? Will you, Daddy? Will you?'

'It's going to be dark by the time we get there, Nikky,' Lukas said, kneeling down to talk to the little boy eye to eye. 'So that would be a no,' he added, never afraid to use a firm hand with Nico—unlike her.

Nico's chin dropped comically to his chest. 'But Daddy, I want to. I've been dreaming about it for hours and hours.'

'To be dreaming about it, you would have had to be asleep,' Lukas pointed out, tucking a finger under Nico's chin and lifting his face to his. 'And not a lot of sleeping has been going on, as I recall.'

'But Daddy…' Nico employed his wheedling voice.

'But Nikky…' Lukas said, mimicking the little boy and making him giggle. 'How about this—if you do as you're told and sleep on the plane now and when we get to the villa tonight, without any more arguments, I promise to take you on the slides first thing in the morning.'

'Really?' Nico asked, his eyes widening with awestruck pleasure, and Bronte's heart became so large she was surprised it didn't burst right out of her chest.

Lukas stood up and looked down at his older son as he continued to soothe the baby on his shoulder. 'Have I ever broken a promise?' Lukas asked, his voice solemn.

Nico shook his head furiously.

'So do we have a deal?' Lukas said.

Nico nodded, just as furiously.

Lukas reached out his free hand and they shook on it together, the poignant father-son bonding moment making Bronte's swollen heart start to choke her. How this man could ever have believed he wouldn't make a brilliant husband and father was beyond her.

Happy tears leaked out of her eyes, which she brushed away before either of them could see them. Because that would simply lead to another poignant father-son bonding moment about how silly Mummy was—for crying about nothing.

But it wasn't nothing to her—it was everything.

'Now, go to sleep and I'll see you in the morning.' Lukas kissed his son's forehead and tucked the sheet around him.

The little boy rolled over and murmured sleepily, 'Yes, Daddy, I'm going to dream about the water slides.'

Lukas chuckled, his throat suddenly raw as he switched off the light and walked out of Nico's room.

Daddy.

Who would ever have thought that one word would come to mean so much to him?

While walking back through the beachside villa towards the bedroom suite—and Bronte—he sent up a few silent words of thanks to his twin and to Darcy O'Hara.

Not just for the gift of Nico, but for everything his life

had become in the last year since their son, his son and Bronte had come into it.

Colourful, chaotic and crazy wonderful.

I hope you can be happy, Alexei, wherever you are, and you can forgive me, Darcy, for once doubting you, knowing that Bronte and I will always love and cherish Nico like our own.

He stepped into the suite and Bronte's head lifted. Their eyes connected and his heartbeat slowed and strengthened. Her lips stretched in a sweet smile. And he felt it echo in the strong steady beats of his heart.

His younger son's dark head lay nestled against her arm, his tiny fist resting against her bare breast, while his lips twitched around her nipple as he attempted to continue nursing even though he was obviously fast asleep.

The rush of blood to his groin was swift and predictable and kind of mortifying. It was probably perverse to find the sight of her nipple while she fed his child so damned erotic. And it was going to be uncomfortable tonight. Once they'd gotten the baby to bed, she would need her sleep too. She had to be tired. No matter how much money you threw at the problem, travelling with two small children was exhausting.

'Did you get Nico to bed okay?' she asked, yawning, as he lifted the baby out of her arms and onto his shoulder.

'Of course—we made a deal,' he said as he patted his younger son's back. He absorbed the warm weight and inhaled the comforting smell of baby shampoo and milk. The baby delivered a satisfying belch. 'Why don't you get into bed,' he said, 'while I put him down?'

'Mmm, thanks.' She stretched, yawning again. And he forced himself to turn away and walk out of the room and not get fixated on the sight of her plump, reddened nipple pouting at him.

Bronte would fall asleep as soon as her head hit the pillow, which would make it that much easier to get his arousal under control when he climbed into bed with her.

He took his time settling his younger son into his crib, the inevitable rush of love and protectiveness helping to distract him from thoughts of his wife's lush body in the room next door.

The inappropriate erection had mercifully wilted and he was congratulating himself on his control when he walked back into the dark bedroom ten minutes later. The sultry breeze off the Indian Ocean drifted in from the open terrace doors, ruffling the dark silhouette of the palm fronds that framed the villa's deck.

Moonlight shimmered on the water outside as he stripped off his clothes, but as he took off his boxers the shadows in the room shifted.

Bronte sat up in the bed, the thin sheet settling into her lap, her naked body and all those delicious curves clearly visible as the moonlight gilded them with a silvery glow.

The blood charged straight back into his groin.

'Why the heck aren't you asleep?' he demanded, his voice hoarse with desire, and no small amount of frustration, as the unruly erection became so stiff it hurt.

'Because it's not past my bedtime yet,' she said, the teasing tone tempered by the husky note of arousal. 'And I've been waiting for you. What took you so long?'

'I was waiting for you to go to sleep,' he said, feeling a little ridiculous as he climbed into bed and grasped her waist to tug her under him. 'So I could do the decent thing—and not ravage you tonight.'

She laughed, the throaty hum making every one of his pulse points pound.

You little minx, I am so going to make you pay for this.

He ravaged the sensitive skin of her neck, all his good intentions burnt away in the firestorm of lust.

'How about I make a deal with you?' she said, shuddering as he flicked his thumb over the slick nub of her clitoris. 'I'll let you do the decent thing *after* you've ravished me.'

'You're on,' he murmured, his voice raw with passion and purpose.

Her delighted laugh turned into a broken sob as he cradled her hips, thrust deep...

And found his way home.

* * * * *

MILLS & BOON

Coming next month

CONSEQUENCE OF
THE GREEK'S REVENGE
Trish Morey

'Going somewhere, Athena?'

Breath hitched in her lungs as every nerve receptor in her body screeched in alarm. Alexios!

How did he know she was here?

She wouldn't turn around. She wouldn't look back, forcing herself to keep moving forwards, her hand reaching for the door handle and escape, when his hand locked on her arm, a five fingered manacle, and once again she tasted bile in her throat, reminding her of the day she'd thrown up outside his offices. The bitter taste of it incensed her, spinning her around.

'Let me go!' She tried to stay calm, to keep the rising panic from her voice. Because if he knew she was here, he must surely know why, and she was suddenly, terribly, afraid. His jaw was set, his eyes were unrepentant, and they scanned her now, as if looking for evidence, taking inventory of any changes. There weren't any, not that anyone else might notice, though she'd felt her jeans grow more snug just lately, the beginnings of a baby bump.

'We need to talk.'

'No!' She twisted her arm, breaking free. 'I've got nothing to say to you,' she said, rubbing the place where his hand had been, still scorchingly hot like he had used a searing brand against her skin, rather than just his fingers.

'No?' His eyes flicked up to the brass plate on near the door, to the name of the doctor in obstetrics. 'You didn't think I might be interested to hear that you're pregnant with my child?'

Continue reading
CONSEQUENCE OF
THE GREEK'S REVENGE
Trish Morey

Available next month
www.millsandboon.co.uk

COMING SOON!

We really hope you enjoyed reading this book. If you're looking for more romance, be sure to head to the shops when new books are available on

Thursday
4th October

To see which titles are coming soon, please visit
millsandboon.co.uk

MILLS & BOON

LET'S TALK
Romance

For exclusive extracts, competitions
and special offers, find us online:

f facebook.com/millsandboon

◉ @millsandboonuk

𝕏 @millsandboon

Or get in touch on 0844 844 1351*

For all the latest titles coming soon, visit
millsandboon.co.uk/nextmonth